"I don't understand."

Meghan pushed Replay to watch the video again, but seeing it the second time didn't alleviate the horror she felt. Two people ripped through her cabana, digging through her desk, her closet....

"They took this video of themselves trashing your room," Alex said. "They were here. This video doesn't show enough to be able to identify them, but they were here last night."

Which meant she had to question all the other things that had happened over the past couple of weeks. Had they really been nothing more than coincidences? She shook her head. None of this made any sense.

"Why would someone do this?" she asked.

"They sent the video to your father, to prove to him that they could get to him."

Her mouth suddenly felt dry as cotton. "How do you know my father?"

Meghan looked at her Texas cowboy and rubbed her temples as a thousand questions swam through her head. One begged to be asked. "Who *are* you?"

Books by Lisa Harris

Love Inspired Suspense

Final Deposit
Stolen Identity
Deadly Safari

LISA HARRIS

is a Christy Award finalist and the winner of the Best Inspirational Suspense Novel for 2011 from *RT Book Reviews*. She has more than twenty novels and novella collections in print. She and her family have spent over ten years living as missionaries in Africa, where she has homeschooled, led a women's group and runs a non-profit organization that works alongside their church-planting ministry. The ECHO Project works in southern Africa promoting Education, Compassion, Health and Opportunity, and is a way for her to "speak up for those who cannot speak for themselves…the poor and helpless, and see that they get justice." (*Proverbs* 31: 8–9).

When she's not working she loves hanging out with her family, cooking different ethnic dishes, photography and heading into the African bush on safari. For more information about her books and life in Africa visit her website, at www.lisaharriswrites.com, or her blog, at www.myblogintheheartofafrica.blogspot.com. For more information about The ECHO Project, please visit www.theechoproject.org.

DEADLY SAFARI

LISA HARRIS

HARLEQUIN LOVE INSPIRED SUSPENSE

Recycling programs
for this product may
not exist in your area.

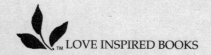

™ LOVE INSPIRED BOOKS

ISBN-13: 978-0-373-44589-9

DEADLY SAFARI

Copyright © 2014 by Lisa Harris

www.Harlequin.com

Printed in U.S.A.

The heavens proclaim the glory of God. The skies display his craftsmanship. Day after day they continue to speak; night after night they make him known. They speak without a sound or word; their voice is never heard. Yet their message has gone throughout the earth, and their words to all the world.

—*Psalms* 19:1–4

Dedicated to all the sweet children I've met,
like Nathi, who've changed my life forever.

ONE

Meghan Jordan lay on her stomach against the thick African grass, steadying the video camera between both hands. This morning, Kibibi, with her sandy-brown coat, had ventured briefly from her den only to disappear again. With her four lion cubs already over a month old, it wouldn't be much longer until she introduced them to the pride. All they had to do now was wait.

Her second camera operator and editor, Kate, handed her a bottle of water from the Jeep's cooler before crouching back down beside her. "What do you think?"

Meghan mulled over the question. "I think that creating a documentary is far less glamorous than I once thought."

"Yeah, well, I figured that one out after the first week."

Meghan smiled as she unscrewed the top of the water bottle, her eyes still on the entrance of the den where Kibibi had moved her cubs six days ago. Unglamorous, maybe, but completely worth it. Eight months as a part of the reserve's conservation program had given them full access to the pride, including the recent birth of Kibibi's four cubs. Statistics showed that 80 percent of all lion cubs died within the first two years, but so far, all of Kibibi's cubs were thriving. They'd already been waiting five weeks to get footage of the lioness finally introducing her cubs to their father. She'd wait another five weeks if she had to.

"Samuel's in the Jeep, keeping his eye on a female black rhino that just wandered into the area."

Meghan frowned. "If she scares away Kibibi, that rhino and I are going to have words."

"I'm more worried about the rhino's bad temper and what it might think about us edging in on its territory."

"Don't worry. Their eyesight is worse than their temper."

"So what does that mean exactly?" Kate asked. "That I hope it won't be able to see me when I have to start running for the nearest tree?"

"As long as you're actually able to scale one of these trees, you'll be fine."

"Right." Kate eyed the nearest Jackalberry tree shooting fifty feet into the air, then shook her head. "I'm not sure which would be worse. Tangling with a rhino or being forced to scale that."

Movement from the tall yellow grass drew Meghan's attention back to the den. Kibibi emerged cautiously with one of the cubs in her mouth.

Bingo. "We've got them."

Meghan lifted up her camera. Samuel was going to have to worry about the rhino for them. She had to focus on getting the last of the footage she needed.

Kibibi took a guarded step forward.

They were either moving on to another den or, as Meghan hoped, finally joining up with the rest of the pride. She held the camera steady, her adrenaline rushing again, while Kate snapped still footage. She could try to script the document down to the smallest detail, but in the end, the wildlife—especially the predators she was documenting—always had the final say. What happened next was up to Kibibi.

The lioness stopped a few feet from the den, her body alert to the scene around her. Something familiar stirred within Meghan. There was nothing like being out in the bush. The never-ending velds bordered by thick forests had become her second home. Here was the one place she'd found that made the stress of the real world disappear—like her other role as the daughter of a diplomat who had recently been appointed ambassador.

The subtle scent of cigarette smoke jerked her attention away from her work.

She nudged Kate with her elbow, her gaze still on Kibibi, who stood still at the top of the ridge outside the den. "Do you smell that?"

"Yeah. All we need now is a fire to set this grass ablaze."

The roar of a second vehicle to their east broke through the stillness of the bush, followed by a deep snort behind her. The rhino. Meghan jerked her head around and peered into the thick brush. That rhino would stomp right over them if they weren't careful. Twenty feet away, Samuel, their driver, sat alert in the Jeep with a safari hat perched on his head and a rifle in his hand.

Meghan glanced back toward Kibibi's den, but she'd already missed her chance for any new footage. The lioness had vanished.

Frustrated, she scanned the thick brush, scattered with spiny tree trunks and limbs covered in green leaves, and spotted the second vehicle as it bridged the gap between them. Her stomach twisted as the second

Jeep moved in between the female rhino and her baby, pushing the mother toward them.

"We need to move now," Kate shouted.

Meghan shoved her camera into the bag and snapped the flap shut. What in the world was the driver doing? Samuel's gun fired behind them in an attempt to scare the rhino back into the thick brush as Kate ran ahead of her for Samuel and the Jeep.

But Meghan's route was cut off as the rhino gave another warning snort, signaling it was about to charge. Meghan's heart pounded. Two tons of rhino wasn't something to tangle with. She weighed her options. Behind her the bush was too thick to negotiate. The only open routes were either toward the baby rhino or up a tree a dozen feet to her right.

As she started to run toward the tree, the second Jeep accelerated past the mother rhino, slowing down briefly beside her. The driver shouted at her to get in. Meghan didn't have time to think. Grabbing the strap of the camera case tightly between her fingers, she swung up onto the passenger side of the vehicle as the rhino charged.

The driver pushed on the accelerator. "How fast can they run?"

"I'd suggest we don't stick around to find out."

Meghan ducked as the tall grass whipped against her face and arms from the sides of the open Jeep. Branches snapped beneath them, but they were beginning to lengthen the distance from the rhino. A second later, her driver hightailed it through a wide opening in the bush to safety.

He glanced at the rearview mirror. "I think we lost her."

As the Jeep came to a stop, Meghan fought to catch her breath. Chest still heaving, she glanced at the stranger beside her wearing a black Stetson, Spanish-style boots, a Western shirt and a belt buckle the size of Texas.

She blinked twice. Who was this guy? "Do you realize how close we both just came to getting killed? If she'd gotten close enough, that rhino could have flipped this Jeep."

He shot her a weak smile. "And I thought I just saved your life."

"You think you saved my life?" Seriously? Meghan's fingers gripped the side of the Jeep. "You're the one who got between that mama and her baby and caused this whole fiasco. You can't just drive where you please—not in a wildlife reserve. In case you hadn't realized it, you're not in Texas anymore."

"Thanks for the tip, but I figured that out a few hours ago. We don't exactly have giraffes and baboons in my part of the world."

"Just longhorns and tumbleweeds?" she countered.

"I suppose we've got a few of those back on the ranch." He pulled off his hat, revealing a pair of striking blue eyes that managed to cut through a layer of her frustration. "But I really am sorry."

He might be good-looking, but she wasn't willing to be charmed. Even saying sorry in that thick Southern drawl of his wouldn't bring Kibibi out of her den today or return the wasted hours they'd spent waiting for the lioness's appearance.

"I guess I should introduce myself. I'm Alex Markham."

"My new assistant?" Meghan swallowed hard. Mr. Cowboy wasn't at all what she'd expected. "You were supposed to arrive yesterday."

"I apologize. I missed my flight out of Amsterdam."

"My boss assured me you could handle the work. What do you know about filming wildlife and making documentaries?"

"Apparently enough for your boss to give me this job."

She frowned, still unimpressed. If he had any real credentials, he'd have mentioned them. The way he was dodging the question seemed to indicate that he had no direct experience at all. Surely he wasn't serious. She'd asked for a film student, not some Texas ranch hand.

She let out a sharp humph. The last thing she needed right now was an unqualified assistant. She'd come a long way from her days as school-newspaper editor at her high school. Since then, she'd moved on to producing short films and online promotional pieces for businesses. The opportunity to make this wildlife documentary held with it the power to propel her further into the world of film, but she needed this footage—and a qualified replacement assistant—to pull it all together.

A twig snapped in the distance. She stared out into the bush, looking for movement. She'd have to deal with Mr. Lone Star later, because something wasn't right. Someone else was out here.

She turned back to him, her brow furrowed. "Do you smoke?"

"Smoke?" The question clearly caught him off guard. "No. Why?"

"I want you to drive back to the spot where you picked me up."

He shook his head as if she was crazy. "In case you forgot, there was a very unhappy rhino back there that I, for one, would prefer to avoid running into again."

"And in case you forgot, an assistant is supposed to assist. Are you going to drive or do I need to?"

Alex hesitated briefly, then spun the vehicle around and headed back toward the clearing.

Meghan leaned into the seat, battling nerves that had settled in the pit of her stomach. If the mystery smoker wasn't Mr. Cowboy, then who was he? And what had he been doing in the middle of nowhere with no one but Meghan's crew, an angry rhino and a litter of lion cubs in range?

Alex knew he'd blown their introduction the moment Meghan jumped into the Jeep. The scowl on her face communicated clearly that he'd failed the first test miserably. He strummed his fingers against the steering wheel, then swerved to avoid a reddish termite mound sticking out of the uneven terrain.

He glanced at her again. Khaki shorts, army-green T-shirt and hiking boots were topped off with a straw sun hat and sunglasses to block the South African sun. She looked tough and capable, not at all like someone in need of protection. But protecting her was exactly why he was there.

His father's pleas reverberated in his mind. *It's a favor for an old army buddy of mine, Ambassador Jordan. He's received threats on his life in connection with upcoming local elections in the country where he serves. In the last threat, they mentioned his daughter. Said that they know where she is. She won't accept a security detail, so you'd have to be discreet. It would just be until the elections are over....*

Sending threats to an American ambassador was a risky move from someone within the opposing party— and so far the threat hadn't been backed up by anything credible—but Alex understood Ambassador Jordan's determination to not take any chances when it came to his daughter's life. Alex knew all too well the way it could crush a man when he failed to protect the ones he loved. The ambassador was wise to take precautions—wiser than Alex had been.

In the end, though, it wasn't just his past griefs or his decade in law enforcement, dedicated to the pursuit of justice, that made him take this assignment. No, his coming had little to do with Meghan. It was the chance to revisit his mother's homeland—something that had been gnawing at the back of his mind—that had eventually clinched the deal.

A flood of memories, untapped for years, rushed over him. As an eleven-year-old, he'd watched the kids walk by in their school uniforms in front of his grandparents' house. He remembered his *ouma* feeding him milk tarts and hunting with his *oupa*. They'd passed away years ago, but he still missed them. Just like he missed his mother.

He shoved the unwanted memories aside. He needed to find out what was going on.

"What are you after?"

"I'm not sure." She stared straight ahead at the narrow, open path through the bush leading back toward where he'd first noticed the rhino. "Something isn't right. We've had issues with poachers, and I need to ensure that they're not back."

Poachers?

Alex wove through the uneven terrain. Just what they needed—another complication. Nothing like throwing a firecracker into the mix of an already explosive situation.

He slowed down as the bush opened up around them. A giraffe lumbered in the distance before stopping to graze. Alex didn't let the peaceful scene distract him.

He was used to the occasional cattle rustlers back on his father's ranch, but even he knew enough to realize that rhino poaching was a serious and often deadly business.

"Stop here."

Alex pushed on the brakes, not sure whether or not he wanted to get out from the relative safety of the Jeep. He'd had enough wildlife encounters for one day.

The only other animal he could see was a harmless-looking zebra grazing in the distance. "Are you sure it's safe to walk around here?"

"You don't need to worry. The rhino we encountered is probably at least a half a mile from here by now. She was as nervous as we were."

"But does she have friends? That's what I want to know."

Meghan laughed for the first time. "It's possible, but most of them will keep their distance if they hear us, unless you have another bright idea about getting between a mother and her babies. Don't forget, there is the lion you scared away in this area, too. We were filming Kibibi and her cubs this morning right over there." She pointed to a clump of grass covering up a small inlet.

"They're the subject of the documentary, right?"

"That's right."

"You think poachers have been out here looking for them?"

"Maybe. More likely, the rhino was their target. Just look for anything that might confirm someone else was out here."

Besides their own footsteps through the dry brush and a few birds chirping, the afternoon was still.

Alex started walking parallel to her, hoping he didn't come across as knowing what he was doing. After ten years as a Texas Ranger, investigative tactics had become like second nature. "You knew I was coming, right?"

"Yes. I was just expecting someone a bit more academic and less..."

"Like a cowboy?" He tugged on the edge of his silver belt buckle. Maybe he should have opted for the safari look.

"That's one way to say it."

She pressed her hand against the top of her head to secure the hat covering her dark blond hair as a breeze blew it back slightly, revealing the handful of freckles sprinkled across her tanned face. She wasn't the only one surprised by appearances. He'd expected more of a bookish-looking grad student from the snapshot her father had sent him. Instead, she was surprisingly pretty. Not his type, maybe, but very pretty. Not that it mattered. Between the time he needed to deal with his father's failing health and his ambition of being captain for the Texas Rangers one day, a relationship at the moment didn't exactly fit into the equation.

Especially since Shannon.

Losing her had convinced him that service to God and country were all he needed in his life.

Shoving aside his thoughts, he continued searching while trying to avoid the spindly thorns covering half the vegetation. The terrain reminded him of going out into the bush with his grandfather, a memory he'd carried with him from childhood, making the landscape feel surprisingly familiar.

Something caught his eye. He took out an empty gum wrapper from his back pocket and picked up a cigarette butt, wishing he had his equipment. "This must be what you were smelling. Looks like someone was stupid enough to almost burn down half this reserve."

"It's still smoldering." Meghan took the gum wrapper and cigarette from him. "This isn't the first time they've been here. The authorities found the same brand of cigarette where some poachers killed a male rhino six weeks ago."

"Could be a coincidence."

"Could be."

"What would they want with a small reserve like this one?"

"Forty-thousand-plus dollars a rhino horn is enough motivation for them to strike wherever they want."

Alex let out a low whistle. "Pretty impressive. But for someone making that kind of money, standing around and smoking while they wait for the rhino to show up seems a little low-tech. I seem to remember reading that poachers have been known to sweep in using helicopters like some high-tech black-ops scenario."

"You make it sound like a scene from some action movie. There are basically two kinds of poachers," Meghan said as she headed back toward the Jeep. "Those who come on foot or Jeep and simply shoot the rhino. Or the ones like you mentioned who use more high-tech methods, weapons and powerful knockout drugs. They can be in and out in a matter of minutes, severing the horn and leaving the rhino to bleed to death. We've already lost two out of eight at this reserve in the past three months."

"Skilled hunters driven by financial gain and greed." He slid into the passenger seat beside her.

"This is what you get when people are willing to pay more than the price of gold for a horn on the illegal market. Estimates are that they're killing an average of one rhino every day. And, thanks to your sudden arrival, they missed their chance to get our rhino today." She caught his gaze as she stepped on the gas and started for the lodge. "Who knows? You might be worth having around after all."

Alex slid his sunglasses back on, then grabbed the metal bar of the Jeep as she followed the trail around a curve through the thick bush, wondering exactly what he'd gotten into. If she was determined to track down a team of deadly poachers, then babysitting Meghan Jordan might turn out to be much harder than he'd anticipated.

Maybe he should have ignored his father's insistence that he come. The last time he'd taken any real time off had been months ago, and Africa wasn't exactly what he'd had in mind for his next vacation. A few days on a quiet island in the Caribbean sounded more to his liking. One day soon he was going to find himself a place where there were no people, no responsibilities and no damsels in distress.

But that day wasn't today.

"Alex…" Meghan's frantic voice broke into his thoughts as she pumped the brake pedal beside him. "I can't slow down."

"Try the emergency brake."

She lunged for the handle, but it was already too late. Alex felt a sharp jolt as the Jeep plunged forward and smashed into the thick base of a baobab tree.

For a moment, there was nothing but silence. Then the distinct call of a bird broke through the eerie quiet of the bush. Alex tried to absorb what had just happened. The realization they weren't going to stop…the ensuing adrenaline rush…the final impact…

He turned to Meghan, who was starting to move. "You okay?"

"I think so. I just rammed my knee into the dashboard." She rubbed a spot on her knee. More than likely she was going to have a nasty bruise by morning. "What about you?"

"I'm okay."

He undid his seat belt, then slowly eased out of the vehicle, alert for any signs of their rhino or any other predatory creature he'd prefer not to tangle with. At least nothing seemed broken, though he'd probably be a bit stiff in the morning. They'd been lucky. It could have been a whole lot worse. If the vehicle had flipped and they'd been thrown out... He shook his head. He wasn't even going to go there.

He moved around to the front of the Jeep to assess the damage. The entire front end was smashed against the tree. Even if it could be fixed, it was going to be a massive repair job. Alex rubbed his temples, wishing he could erase the headache beginning to pulse. There was another, bigger issue to consider. Even though Meghan had driven out in a different Jeep, he couldn't discount the possibility that the accident was connected to the threats against her life.

TWO

Alex kicked the side of the bumper that now sat askew. Then, pushing the frustration down, he forced himself to think logically, like the investigator he was. "Who has access to the lodge's vehicles?"

"Access?" Meghan hobbled to the front of the vehicle to make her own assessment, her knee clearly painful. "Everyone, I suppose—or rather, the small number of people who are in the area. They're not exactly kept under tight security. We're in the bush, twenty minutes from the nearest town. Except for poaching, crime isn't exactly a huge issue here."

"And at night?"

"They're not locked up, if that's what you mean. They sit in the parking lot when they aren't being used in the bush or in for maintenance. The terrain is rough on them, so it's a lot of work to keep them running."

"So, in other words, anyone who wanted to could have access to them."

She rested her hands against her hips and caught his gaze. "Are you implying this wasn't an accident? Because if you are, that's absolutely ridiculous. Like I said, the terrain is rough. Mechanical issues with the vehicles are the norm rather than the exception."

"I'm not implying anything. I just…"

He closed his mouth, reminding himself that he wasn't allowed to say more to warn her about the chance of danger. It wasn't the first time he'd questioned Ambassador Jordan's explicit instructions. He'd prefer to simply lay out the entire truth for Meghan. *By the way, your father is worried someone is trying to kill you. And while you think I'm your new assistant, the truth is that your father just convinced me to blow my vacation time by working as your bodyguard and talked your boss into playing along so you wouldn't suspect the truth. Hope you don't mind.*

He looked to where she stood. Brow furrowed. Questioning. No matter what he would like to say, he was pretty certain her father had been right about one thing. While he might not be her choice of assistant on her documentary team, she'd definitely send him packing if she realized he was here as her personal guard detail. From what he'd already seen, the girl had just enough spunk and stubbornness to make her believe she could handle things on her own. Which put it back on his shoulders to find a way to keep her out of trouble whether she wanted him to or not.

"You know, I'm sorry." He tried to erase the look of worry from his expression. "It's been one of these weeks. I missed my flight out of Amsterdam, which resulted in them losing my bag. Then there was a flat tire on the way here, and now all of this…."

She slammed her open door shut with her hip. "Today might just be your lucky day after all."

He leaned against the side of the vehicle and shot her a surprised look. "Lucky? Right. I always consider myself lucky when I'm chased by a rhino before wrapping a vehicle around a tree."

"Think of it this way. We were scheduled to take this vehicle out today." Alex kept his expression neutral, not visibly reacting to the information even as he mentally stored it away. "But Samuel noticed that the radio wasn't working, so we swapped out vehicles." She smiled at him. He wasn't sure if she was flirting with him or simply being sarcastic. "So if it weren't for the rhino incident, I'd be back safe and sound at the lodge, but you'd be here by yourself with no idea how to get back and no radio. Lucky you, though, I'm here, and I know the way back to the lodge."

"That's a very…optimistic way of looking at it." He had to laugh. So Meghan was one of those eternal optimists? "What now? There's no radio, but you have to have a cell phone on you, right?"

"A cell phone? No. Even if I did, there isn't any service out here."

Great. He glanced back at the Jeep. "Which is why you use radios."

"Precisely."

"Here's another crazy question." He hesitated, hoping he didn't sound as worried as he felt. "What kind of predators might show up, besides our favorite rhino and a handful of poachers? Because this wreck isn't going anywhere."

"Don't you have predators back in Texas?"

"I've tangled with a coyote or two."

He tried to play down his concern, but his unease went far beyond what might be hiding on the other side of the bushes. Not only did she see the cup half-full, she was unaware that they faced any problem other than getting out of the bush. He was looking at an entirely different scenario. Maybe he was reading things into the situation, but if the vehicle had been sabotaged, someone had just sent a very clear message that they could get to her.

Something rustled behind him in the bushes. Alex pressed his back against the vehicle, ready to grab Meghan and bolt the pair of them up the nearest tree if necessary.

"It's okay." Meghan laughed. "It's just an impala."

"An impala."

"An antelope. A lot of people mistake them for deer, but they actually come from different families. An impala's color is more reddish-brown and they have permanent horns—"

"I know what an impala is."

"Sorry."

"No, I'm sorry."

He held up his hand. He shouldn't have snapped, but he couldn't take any chances if someone had just tried to kill her. Nor was he thrilled about being out in the bush unarmed, where there were predators that would be more than happy to have him for dinner. He knew enough to realize that the hunter could quickly become the hunted. And unless someone came to their rescue, they were going to have to walk back to the lodge. At this point he wasn't even sure which direction it was.

She took a step and winced, reminding him of their other problem. They were going to have to walk, and she clearly wasn't going to make it far. The discoloration on her knee was already beginning to show.

"From the looks of it, you're not going anywhere, either. At least not quickly."

So much for outrunning the next animal that decided to have some fun with them.

"I'll be fine." She forced a smile. "And besides, Kate and Samuel know I'm out here. They probably assumed you drove me back to the lodge, but once they realize we're not there, they'll come looking for us. They know the area where we are, so it shouldn't take them long to find us."

He wasn't convinced. "Not to be a pessimist or anything, but what if they don't show up? Do you really think you can walk back to the lodge?

"Do you always worry like this?"

"Yes."

His caution tended to go hand in hand with a job of hunting down the bad guys. For the past thirteen months he'd been after Dimitri Stamos, who'd left six people dead in his latest crime spree. Being on the alert for danger came as easily as breathing and was just as necessary in his life. He knew how to track and hunt down criminals, but trekking through the bush eluding wild animals—and possibly dangerous humans, too—was different.

He glanced down at her again, in her khaki shorts and boots, looking completely at home in the middle of the African bush—and compellingly attractive despite his best intentions not to notice. What he couldn't avoid noticing was her refusal to back down.

"There is nothing to worry about." She didn't seem to notice his conflicted mood. "I've been working out here for months, and while we typically go out with a gun, we've never had to use it."

"Until today," he reminded her.

"It was a warning shot. That rhino was more afraid of us than we would ever be of him."

Right.

"How far to the lodge?"

"Two, maybe three miles at the most."

Alex frowned. This wasn't going to work. "You can barely walk."

She took another step and forced a smile, though the pain radiating in her eyes was clear. "I'm fine."

"No, you're not."

He tried to formulate a plan with the little information he had. Staying in the open Jeep after dark seemed more foolish than prudent. Walking through the bush with the chance of encountering a leopard or lion seemed just as foolish. Somehow he needed to come up with a plan C.

"What do you think you'll do when something starts chasing you and you can't outrun it?" he asked.

"Like I said, in my experience, most animals are going to be more afraid of us than we are of them." She glanced at the baobab the Jeep sat wrapped around. "Or there's always the nearest tree."

Maybe so, but he wasn't looking forward to taking his chances. "How long until dark?"

She glanced at her watch. "Forty-five minutes… maybe a bit less."

At a brisk pace they could make it—if they didn't get eaten along the way. And if he helped her. He hesitated, then bridged the gap between them.

"I say we take our chances and walk, but you're going to lean on me."

"Really, it's not that bad." She took another step, then reached down to rub the bruised spot on the side of her knee that was already starting to swell.

"Right. You need to get off the leg and ice it, but since you can't do that, you're going to have to let me help you."

She looked up at him with those big brown eyes of hers took another step, winced, then stopped. "Fine."

He wrapped his arm around her waist, wishing her hair didn't smell like lavender and that her lashes didn't go on forever when she looked up at him. He'd figured she'd be intelligent. He hadn't planned on her being such a...distraction.

The only solution to the problem, as far as he could see, was to tell her the truth. If she knew he was here doing a favor for one of his father's old army buddies, who happened to be her own somewhat-estranged father, she'd be furious. Attraction definitely wouldn't be a problem, since she wouldn't let him within five miles of her. But if he blew his cover and told her the truth, he wouldn't be able to protect her. And with the way things were spiraling out of control in the current election, and after what he'd seen today, he tended to believe that her life really was in danger. She needed him here, whether she knew it or not. And that meant he couldn't do anything to drive her away.

Alex shifted his gaze back to the uneven path, pushing aside his straying thoughts as he tried to focus on the situation at hand. All he needed to do right now was get them back to the lodge in one piece. "Which way?"

"That way." She nodded toward their right, then stopped. "I forgot my bag."

He grabbed her camera bag out of the Jeep, waited until she'd adjusted it on her shoulder, then wrapped his arm around her waist again. She looked up at him before slowly wrapping her arm around his waist. The wind blew a strand of her hair across his face. He brushed it aside, tightened his grip, then started walking.

There was something about her that intrigued him.

Okay, more than just one thing. Meghan Jordan was a filmmaker, seemingly as comfortable in the African bush as most women were at a shopping mall. She was intelligent, strong-minded and undeniably beautiful. Exactly what he wasn't looking for.

Alex swallowed hard. He really needed a distraction.

Meghan took another step and tried to ignore the pain.

"You okay?"

She nodded at his question, avoiding his gaze. Her knee was already swelling, but while she might need a distraction from the pain, Mr. Lone Star wasn't what she had in mind.

Today, she'd looked forward to filming some of the final scenes with Kibibi and her cubs. Instead, Alex had torpedoed into her life, bringing with him a string of disasters. He'd barely been here an hour, and he'd ticked off a rhino and gotten them stranded out in the bush.

All right, maybe it hadn't been his fault that the Jeep had malfunctioned, but still, the vehicle they'd been driving was now wrapped around the trunk of a baobab tree. Nothing like that had happened to her *before* he'd shown up.

She should be mad at him, but instead, having him so close was wreaking havoc with her equilibrium. Which left her wondering what bothered her the most. The fact that she'd just been sent an assistant who more than likely didn't know anything about the African bush, or the fact that she couldn't ignore the feel of his arm wrapped tightly around her waist.

She searched for something to say to break the awkward silence between them as they followed the narrow trail bordered by the overgrown forest. "You do know the most important rule of the bush, don't you?"

"The most important?" He hesitated. "I'm not sure."

"Make sure you look both up and down."

"Meaning?"

"Down to avoid any holes and snakes. Up to check for any unwelcome predators."

She felt the muscles in his arm tense and suppressed a chuckle. She had no idea where her boss had found this guy, but cowboy or not, he seemed better qualified to lead a hoedown than a trek through the bush.

"Sounds like good advice."

Moments later, she stopped at a rise in the terrain, where forest opened up into a narrow grassland. Even after eight months of working here, she'd yet to tire of the ever-changing landscape and animals that filled its terrain.

"It's beautiful, isn't it?" she said.

"Incredibly."

The sun began to drop in the distance, painting the sky brilliant shades of orange and pink. Acacia trees, with their flat, green tops, sprinkled the horizon. Half a dozen giraffes walked gracefully across the far edge of the open veld.

She pointed toward the left. "Look down there, at the water hole."

A family of elephants had gathered at the water's edge, mamas and babies with their bulky forms casting gray shadows across the tall grasses. This was the one place in the world where she felt safe, alive and whole.

"Do you believe in God?"

He nodded at her question. "'The heavens declare the glory of God and the skies his handiwork.' It's hard not to believe when you see things like this."

She'd always felt the same way. Cell phones, the internet and email always managed to pull her in a million different directions. But standing here, in the quiet stillness of God's creation, everything seemed to move back into perspective.

"Wait a bit longer until darkness settles in and the stars come out. There's nothing like seeing the Milky Way and the Southern Cross light up the sky."

They started walking again. "Do all of the assistants on your project get such personalized attention?"

She didn't quiet her laugh this time as she looked up at him, wondering how he'd become the distraction that had almost erased the pain in her knee. "I can't say that I've ever escorted a cowboy through the bush."

Arm snug around her waist, those dark eyes with a hint of amusement in their depths, this particular cowboy looked incredibly appealing. But she brushed the thought aside. There was no way she was falling for this stranger. There was no way she was falling for anyone, because she'd yet to meet a man who made her feel worthy of being loved. Relationships weren't for her, and that was that.

She dismissed the ridiculous train of thought. They continued walking. Twenty more minutes, thirty tops, and they'd be back at the lodge. In a couple more weeks, the job would be over, and she could send him back to Texas. Which was why, for now, it was time to change the subject.

"Have you ever been to South Africa before?"

"I visited once. Many years ago. My mother was from here."

"So, coming here was more than just a job?"

"You could say that. I've always wanted a reason to return to my mother's homeland."

"You've piqued my interest." She adjusted the grip of her hand around his waist. The fact that they had something in common surprised her. Her father had grown up in Kenya, the son of a missionary, so she'd learned early on the mysterious lure of the the African continent. "Tell me about yourself."

"Me?"

"If we're going to work together," she said, "we might as well get to know each other. Where is your family from?"

"My father owns a ranch in West Texas, but many years ago, shortly after he passed the bar, his father arranged a hunting trip for him north of here near the Zimbabwe border. My mother's father owned the game farm where they hunted. And as they say, the rest is history. They fell in love, had a whirlwind romance, and eventually they married and she followed him to the United States."

"Romantic."

"It was, but she died when I was twelve."

"Do you miss her?"

"Every day."

"Any sisters or brothers?"

"Three older sisters. My father never remarried. I don't think he ever got over losing her. I think it's your turn now. What about you?"

Meghan had realized the moment she'd asked him the first question she'd opened up a can of worms she'd prefer left closed. She loved her father, but their relationship had always been strained. It had been weeks since they'd talked and even longer since they'd seen each other. Explaining that to strangers was difficult.

"My story's a bit more complicated."

"Isn't family always?"

She laughed. She liked him, which bothered her. And he was clearly worried and protective over her safety.

But none of that mattered beyond the short term.

They had been nearly finished with their filming when Jared, her asssistant, came down with a life-threatening case of malaria. Once the filming was wrapped up and the edits finished, she'd never see Alex again.

She switched her mind back to his question. "I'm an only child. Boarding schools for junior high and high school, summers and vacations with my aunt in Southern California. There really isn't much exciting about my life unless you want to start comparing who's visited the most countries or eaten the weirdest food."

"Deep-fried cantaloupe pie at the county fair is about all I have to offer."

She wrinkled her nose. "I think I'd opt for a bag of barbecued Mopani worms before trying a slice of that."

Alex laughed. Maybe the man was actually beginning to relax.

"You mentioned a lot of traveling. Where's home?" he probed.

"I don't really have one. My father's an ambassador. I see him a couple times a year. I love him, but after my mother left him when I was fourteen, things changed between us. It wasn't his fault, though. I don't know a man alive who'd know how to deal with a moody teen while trying to save his part of the world."

Meghan pressed her lips together, wondering why she was baring her heart to a man she'd just met. Even Kate didn't know the details of her relationship with her father, and they'd known each other for months. "The lodge is just over the next ridge. We should be able to see the lights any moment now."

"Tell me about this assignment you've been working on. I was given some details, but still would like to know more."

She let out a sigh, thankful for the change in subject.

"For starters, this is my first big assignment. As you probably already know, it's a documentary in connection with the lodge and the reserve's conservation program, the Chizoba Predator Project. For eight months, we've been tracking a lion family and documenting the dynamics within the pride. Now we're waiting to take the final footage we need, when Kibibi introduces her cubs to their father. It should happen in the next couple weeks."

Meghan stepped into a shallow hole along the path and felt her sore knee twist. She stumbled against him.

"You okay?"

"Yeah. I just need to be careful." She tried to find her balance, then pulled back slightly from his steady grip. "The ground isn't even, and the last thing I need is to sprain something else."

"Make sure you look both up and down."

"Very funny."

He winked at her, only managing to intensify the ridiculous stir of her heart.

"We can stop here for a moment if you need to."

She tried to take another step on her own, felt her knee give and had to press her hands against his chest for balance. He was too close, her emotions too near the surface. Talking about her father always brought with it turmoil from the past. And the handsome cowboy in front of her wasn't helping.

She drew in a deep breath and tried to relax. Something wasn't right. "Do you smell that?"

"What?"

"Cigarette smoke again."

She'd always been sensitive to smells, making her certain this was the same scent she'd noticed earlier today. The same brand the poachers had left. They were out here somewhere. Planning. Tracking. Preparing for another strike. She was certain of it.

The roar of an engine jerked her from her thoughts. She turned toward the noise and felt her breath catch.

"Poachers."

"Who's being paranoid now?" He nudged her with his shoulder. "It's probably just your friends coming to pick you up."

"Maybe." She pulled them off the trail and into the cover of the bush, waiting for the vehicle to emerge. He was probably right, but if not... "My paranoia stems from reality. There was something I didn't mention earlier."

"What's that?"

"The last person who got in the poachers' way was murdered."

THREE

Meghan let her lungs release the air they'd been holding as soon as the familiar form of Samuel appeared in the disappearing light, driving one of the lodge's vehicles. Relief spread through her. She'd been wrong. Which meant no more worrying tonight about poachers, wild predators...or needing Alex's help.

She stepped back onto the trail as Kate jumped from the Jeep and threw her arms around Meghan's neck.

"Whoa, careful." Pain shot through Meghan's knee as she fought to keep her balance. Alex grabbed her shoulders from behind to steady her, but she managed to hobble away from both of them to lean against the front bumper of the Jeep.

"What in the world happened to you?" Kate began. "I've been worried sick. I saw you jump into the other vehicle. I thought you were behind us, but by the time we circled around to check on you, you'd vanished." Kate's gaze shifted from Meghan's bruised leg to Alex. "And who are you?"

"Kate, Samuel," Meghan began. "Meet Alex Markham. He's our new production assistant. Kate works with photography and editing, and Samuel's one of the best trackers you'll find in southern Africa."

"Assistant?" Kate's gaze narrowed.

"I am sorry about what happened earlier. I certainly didn't mean to cause such a commotion." Alex shot Kate a smile, then held out his hand. "It's nice to meet you, Kate. Samuel."

Any traces of frustration on Kate's face disappeared. "It's nice to meet you, too, Mr. Markham."

"Call me Alex."

"Okay…Alex."

Meghan caught Kate's gaze taking in Mr. Lone Star's Stetson, boots, belt buckle and all his charm. She was actually fawning over the man.

Meghan shook her head. He was smooth. She'd give him credit for that. And attractive, if you liked the cowboy type. But the last thing she needed was another complication in her life.

"Yes, Kate, he'll be picking up the slack for Jared."

Her grin had yet to diminish. "Sounds good to me."

"I am glad the two of you are safe, but what about your vehicle?" Samuel didn't seem to notice Kate's gawking stare. "I am assuming that since you are out on foot in the middle of the bush at dusk that something happened to it."

"The brakes on the Jeep gave out," Meghan told him.

"Is that when you hurt your leg?" Kate asked.

"Yes, I smashed it against the dash, but it's nothing. Really."

"I'm not sure about that." Kate studied the bruise in what little light remained. "It's already turning purple."

"It's nothing that a bag of ice and a couple pain pills can't fix."

"And the vehicle?" Samuel asked. "What is the damage there?"

"The front end's banged up pretty badly. It's wrapped around the base of a tree trunk."

Samuel's gaze narrowed. "You know Ian is not going to be happy about another big expense, but at least both of you are okay. That is what really matters."

Meghan caught the concern in Samuel's eyes.

"Meghan tends to be a bit accident-prone," Kate began.

"What kind of accidents?" Alex asked.

"In case you didn't notice, I can hear you both." Meghan frowned as she set her camera down and climbed into the front passenger seat.

Kate slid into the backseat beside Alex. "It is true, Meghan. Either you're accident-prone or maybe you've just had a string of bad luck lately—"

"It was nothing," Meghan countered.

"What kinds of accidents?" Alex repeated.

"For one," Kate began, "two days ago, the side of a hide collapsed while Meghan was inside studying our lion family. All joking aside, it actually could have been very dangerous."

"It collapsed?"

Meghan caught the concern in Alex's voice. "Kate. You shouldn't have brought that up."

"Why not?"

"Because our new assistant has a tendency to worry. He even implied that the brakes on the Jeep went out due to sabotage." The guy was clearly a worrywart. She'd only added to the mess by mentioning the poachers to him. The idea that the poachers might come after her seemed stupid now. The man who'd been killed had been in the wrong place at the wrong time. The chances of it happening again were pretty much zilch.

"Sabotage?" Samuel headed back toward the lodge.

"That does not seem very likely. It is far more probable that the owners are cutting back on costs and missed the vehicle's last scheduled maintenance."

"The owner's facing financial issues?" Alex asked.

"No more than any other lodge when the world economy is down."

"It's one of the reasons he agreed to help with the documentary we're working on," Meghan added. "He's hoping the added exposure will bring in more tourists. Kate and I blog, and post on Facebook and Twitter, everything we do, complete with videos and photos. People love it."

"Have there been any other accidents?" Alex clearly wasn't ready to drop the subject.

"Kate, I'm warning you. Say nothing. Because, Mr. Lone Star, as much as you seem to want there to be, there is no conspiracy going on here. In fact, our days are far less glamorous than most people think, and certainly not dangerous unless you count an occasional encounter with a pack of wild dogs or—like today—a run-in with a rhino. Most of our time is spent out in the bush waiting. No saboteurs, no encounters with poachers, no bad guys waiting in the wings."

A moment later, the lights of the lodge came into view, hopefully putting an end to the conversation for good. Because all Meghan wanted now was a hot shower and a good night's sleep.

She stood up and slid out of the Jeep before Alex or the others could react. "Thanks for the ride, Samuel. I appreciate your coming back for us."

"Where are you going?" Kate asked.

"Back to my chalet. Once I get ahold of a bag of ice and some pain medicine, I plan on crashing. It's been a long day."

"I will talk to Ian about the vehicle and make sure it is brought in."

"Thank you, Samuel."

"And I'll walk you to your cabin."

Meghan took a step forward, then turned back to Alex. "I appreciate your help, really I do, but I'm fine. My knee's feeling better already, and I'm sure you want to get settled."

Alex Markham had managed to wreak havoc with her emotions, and she needed distance to help her regain some perspective.

"Okay, but I think you should get your leg checked out by a professional." He caught her gaze, causing her stomach to flip. "Isn't there a doctor or clinic nearby?"

"He's right, Meghan," Kate added. "You should see a doctor. Just to make sure nothing is broken or torn."

Meghan shook her head. "I'll be fine. It's been a long day, and tomorrow will be just as long. I'll see you all in the morning."

Before anyone could say another word, Meghan started down the paved walkway that ran beside a row of chalets, determined not to limp. Everything she'd said had been true. All she needed was some pain medicine and an ice pack, and she'd be as good as new by morning.

Alex—and Kate, for that matter—was making far too big a deal about nothing.

Something rustled behind the purple flowering bougainvillea hedge to her right. Meghan squinted at the thick climbing vine. There were intermittent spotlights along the path, but clouds had covered up the stars and moon, leaving it too dark to see anything.

Meghan sped up, trying to put as little weight as

possible on her bad leg as she hobbled down the path. She was beginning to see a poacher behind every bush. She shook her head. This was crazy. Alex and his paranoia were rubbing off on her. It was probably nothing more than a bush baby or a monkey looking for a free handout.

Meghan repositioned the strap of her camera bag over her shoulder. She'd been foolish to venture out without her flashlight, but Alex had her completely rattled. How could a man she knew nothing about leave her so flustered? Clearly she'd been out in the bush too long. For the most part, the men who stayed at the lodge were either over sixty or had wives or girlfriends. None of them had garnered a second look from her.

She started down the row of chalets where the staff stayed. Tonight was quiet, as most people were up at the lodge eating dinner.

Meghan stopped. This time she was sure she'd heard something, and whatever it was sounded too big to be a monkey.

"Hello?"

No answer.

She continued down the path, past her chalet, ready to prove to Alex that there was no bogeyman or saboteur—

Meghan froze as the main power switched off, leaving her in total darkness. Without a flashlight, it was almost impossible to see what was ahead of her. She'd wandered too far down the path to be able to find her chalet, but neither did she want to stay where she was. She knew from experience that power outages could potentially last for hours.

She turned back toward the chalets and took an uneasy step forward. Her knee buckled, and she hit the ground full force. Meghan screamed at the impact, felt her head hit something hard, then gave way to the blackness surrounding her.

"Is she always so...?" Alex searched for the right word as Meghan disappeared down the path toward her chalet.

"Bullheaded?" Kate suggested.

"I was thinking more *independent,* but *bullheaded* works."

"Yes, but she's fantastic to work with. She's creative, funny, focused..."

He followed Kate toward the reception area of the lodge that was decorated with woven baskets and life-size wooden carvings of monkeys, turtles and warthogs. A group of tourists were climbing into one of the vehicles, cameras and extra lenses in hand, for a night safari in the bush. There were more people around than he'd expected. And any one of them could be responsible for their crash earlier.

He couldn't worry about that now. He had other things to do. He needed to get the key to his room and check with the airport to see if they would deliver his suitcase tomorrow. Otherwise, the one extra set of clothes he'd packed in his carry-on was going to have to be supplemented by a few souvenir shirts and shorts in the gift shop.

"What's her story?" he asked as they approached the front desk, hoping he might discover something beyond what Meghan had told him.

"Meghan's? She grew up as an only child, divorced parents, boarding schools—she comes by her independence naturally."

He might have just met Meghan, but something about her intrigued him. She was down-to-earth, witty and passionate, which made a refreshing change from most of the women his friends had tried to set him up with lately.

"What about you?" Kate leaned against the polished wooden counter. "We usually eat dinner together about this time in the restaurant. Care to join me and tell me a little more about yourself?"

Alex took his key from the receptionist and weighed his options. Hungry or not, he wasn't here to socialize. His first priority was to keep an eye on Meghan, a task that was proving to be far from easy. Which meant for starters he needed to find out where she was staying. "I'd love to, but jet lag is starting to hit hard. I've got a granola bar and trail mix that will hold me over until tomorrow. Which way to my chalet?"

Kate looked at his key and pointed to her right. "You're number five. The staff chalets are all located straight down that path a hundred yards or so. I'm number two if you need anything."

"And Meghan?" He caught a hint of amusement in her eyes at the question and tried to cover his tracks. "Just in case I need something and can't find you."

"Of course. She's in number seven."

"Great. Thanks."

On his way out, he paused at an aerial photo of the Chizoba Safari Lodge and its adjoining game reserve. Besides the two-dozen luxury chalets with thatched roofs for guests that overlooked the grassy veld, there was a restaurant, bar, day spa, activity center and swimming pool. It was all very impressive. But he wasn't here to enjoy a vacation.

Alex headed in the direction of the chalet where he'd

be staying. Somehow he was going to have to find a way to keep tabs on Meghan without her thinking he was stalking her. Because, in his eyes, everything that had happened today had only confirmed her father's fears.

Halfway down the paved walkway, the power went out, throwing him into pitch darkness. Great. Alex stopped midstride, surprised at how dark it was. No lights meant there was no way he was going to find his cabin. He stood in the middle of the path and made a mental note to carry a flashlight with him if it turned out that power outages were the norm. Which they probably were.

Poachers, charging rhinos, failing brakes… It was as if he'd stepped into a different reality where, on top of everything else, beautiful women like Meghan had somehow managed to yank his heartstrings.

Alex heard the scream from where he stood.

Meghan?

He squinted, but his eyes still hadn't adjusted to the darkness. Silence followed. He didn't have a choice but to try to find her. A dozen yards later, he ran smack-dab into something—or somebody. He heard her scream again as he tripped and landed on the ground beside her.

He rolled onto his side and groaned. "Meghan?"

"Alex? What in the world are you doing here?" Funny. It was the same question he'd asked himself a dozen times the past twelve hours.

"I heard a scream," he answered.

"It was me. Sorry. Just help me up. Please."

"Are you okay?"

"I'm fine. I just…tripped."

"I—"

"Don't say anything."

"I wasn't going to."

"Right."

His arms were still around her as the moon came out from behind the clouds, giving him just enough light so he could see her expression. A mixture of pain and embarrassment filled her eyes.

"You okay? Anything else hurt?"

"No, I don't think so."

He pushed back a strand of hair from her forehead, his other arm still around her waist. "Whoa. You've got a goose egg here."

She felt the spot on the edge of her scalp. "I must have hit my head when I fell."

He found himself not wanting to let go of her as she took a step back.

"What happened?" he asked.

"The lights went out, and like I said, I tripped."

"That's it?"

The lights came back on, this time completely illuminating her face. Wide eyes, furrowed brow, a frown and yet somehow undeniably adorable. He reined in his train of thought.

"As much as I don't want to admit it," she began, "Kate was right. I'm a bit accident-prone."

"So this was just an accident?" He wasn't sure he believed her.

"The lights went out. I tried to make it to my cabin and tripped."

Alex glanced around him. They were past the row of chalets. From what he could see, the path continued on toward the watering hole.

"You're past your cabin."

She started walking back up the path. "You'd think I was paranoid if I told you that I thought someone was following me."

Alex felt a wave of alarm strike. "Meghan, what happened?"

"Nothing. I heard a noise and went to investigate. It was probably just a baboon or someone on their way to their chalet."

"Tell me exactly what you heard."

"I don't know, just some rustling in the bushes. Like I said, it was probably nothing. It's been a long day and I'm tired, which means I'm imagining things. Someone I know has put ideas of sabotage in my head."

"I'm sorry, but it seems a bit coincidental. First the brakes on the Jeep give out, and now you think someone was following you? Not to mention the thing that Kate brought up."

Meghan laughed. "Please, you sound just like my father. He's convinced that there is an evil plot behind everything. The Jeep's brakes failed because the vehicle is old and the mechanic somehow missed it. Nothing more, nothing less."

For a moment he considered simply telling her the truth. It seemed ridiculous to hide things from her, but he had made a promise. He'd call the ambassador tonight, update him on the situation and advise him that Meghan be told what was going on.

She stopped in front of one of the chalets. Number seven.

"This is your place?"

"Home, sweet home."

He moved closer to her and wrapped an arm around her waist as she started up the stairs that looked as if they could use a bit of repair themselves.

"I can get up the stairs on my own."

She pulled back, but he only tightened his grip. "And take the chance of falling again? I don't think so."

"Alex."

"No arguing." He helped her up the stairs and stopped at front of the door before giving her the space she wanted and *he* needed. "I want you to promise me one more thing."

"What is that?"

"Lock your door tonight."

"You're being paranoid again."

"I just want you to be smart—and safe. If there are poachers around, like you said, it's worth being prudent." He caught the doubt in her eyes. "Promise?"

"Promise."

"Good."

He took a step backward—physically and emotionally. He wasn't going to let himself get too attached. Not this time. Not again. His only plan was to keep Meghan safe for the ambassador until the election was over in two weeks, and then he was going to leave.

Until then, maintaining distance would help him do his job effectively. It would make Meghan safer. And it would help him protect the heart he never wanted to put at risk again.

Thirty minutes later, Alex finally got through to her father. "Ambassador Jordan. This is Alex Markham."

"I didn't expect to hear from you so soon. Is my daughter okay?"

"Yes, but now that I'm here, I believe that in order for me to effectively do my job, I need to tell your daughter the truth—"

"No. Please. You promised me you wouldn't tell her anything."

"I don't think you understand, Ambassador. Meghan is...independent. I can and will do everything I can to ensure she is safe, but without her knowledge of who I am and how she's at risk, there is only so much I can do. I can't find a reason to be with her twenty-four hours a day."

"I need you to do this without her knowing." His voice softened. "If she finds out, I'll lose her. I've already dragged her into many dangerous situations. She'll blame me for messing up this job. For always interfering."

"You're not going to lose her, sir. She knows you love her."

"Has something happened to make you think the men who contacted me are making good on their threats?"

"At this point, I'm not sure." Alex hesitated. Everything that had taken place could be explained away as coincidence, just like Meghan believed, but if she was wrong...

"The brakes went out on our vehicle today. She's certain that maintenance missed the problem. The terrain is rough here, and I can't be sure that this was related to the threats you've received."

"But it could be related to the threats, and you know it."

"Either way, let me tell her the truth."

"Not yet. Just promise me you'll take care of her. Because if I lose Meghan, I lose everything. Please, Alex. I'm trusting you to take care of my daughter."

Ice shot through Alex at the memory of another family who had trusted him with their daughter. He'd let that family down. He wouldn't—couldn't—fail again.

"I'll do everything I can to keep Meghan safe, sir. You have my word."

FOUR

Meghan lay wide awake in her bed, listening to the familiar sounds of the African night. Lightning flashed in the distanced, followed by the fierce rumble of thunder sweeping across the terrain. At the moment, she was unsure if it was the light show, her throbbing knee or her growing frustration over what had happened tonight that was keeping her awake.

She couldn't believe she'd gotten so worried about the danger of poachers at the lodge that she'd added a head wound to her twisted knee. It was pure nonsense to believe she was in any personal danger—she never should have let herself believe otherwise.

She rolled over onto her other side, trying to find a more comfortable position. Something tapped against the window. In the darkened room, all she could see were shadows. The wind had picked up. She could hear the branches of the trees creaking above the thatched chalet roof. That was making the tapping noise—a branch.

Tap...tap...tap...

Meghan swallowed hard. Or she could be wrong. Something—or someone—could be outside her chalet.

She tried to shake off the ridiculous thought. She

was being paranoid like Mr. Cowboy. He'd swept in like a tornado, worried about everything and blaming the accident in the Jeep on sabotage. Seriously? The man must have an overactive imagination. The only enemy the reservation had was poachers. With security beefed up after their recent attack, they'd be foolish to strike again. Yes, she'd found the same cigarette butts, but that didn't really mean anything. More than likely hundreds of people smoked that brand. Finding them again was nothing more than another coincidence.

But still…

Meghan rolled over again, then worked to untangle herself from the sheet while trying to tame her nerves. The hide needed to be upgraded—it was hardly surprising that it had collapsed on her. And as for the brakes on the Jeep, she'd heard Samuel mention to Ian just last week that they were going to need to do some repairs on the vehicles. It was only to be expected that the combination of neglect and her clumsiness would equal disaster.

No, recent events were nothing more than a run of bad luck—if she believed in bad luck, which she didn't. Hopefully, it would be a reminder to Ian of the importance of maintenance. He'd become overtaxed with the threat of poachers, hiring extra guards and trying to stay in the black despite the fragile economy, which had led him to cut corners. But even though repairs had fallen by the wayside, she should feel safer knowing the reserve was actually well prepared against potential poachers.

Tap…tap…tap…*crash*…

She flung off her covers and grabbed for her flashlight. Until she figured out what was out there, she wasn't going to be able to sleep. She moved to the window, pushed back the flimsy curtains, then squinted across the dimly lit wooded area surrounding the row of chalets. Mr. Cowboy had stirred her imagination, making her believe whatever was out there was more than just a baboon or one of the dozens of scavenging nocturnal animals.

Meghan peered into the darkness. Shadows danced in the moonlight. Trees swayed in the wind. If she let her imagination run wild, she could easily come up with a dozen unsavory explanations of what might be roaming through the bush. She wouldn't let that happen. There was nothing out there that shouldn't be out there.

But still…

She pulled on a pair of shorts, unlocked the front door, then stepped gingerly out onto the wooden porch. The wind was picking up and the temperature had dropped a few degrees. In the next hour or so, the storm would hit the lodge. That was surely enough to keep away any wannabe poachers. She held her breath for a moment, trying not to make any noise. With her luck lately, the "intruder" would probably turn out to be some cranky old baboon wanting access to the bowl of fruit sitting on her tiny kitchen counter.

She reached down to rub the top of her throbbing knee before walking down the wooden steps leading from the porch, wincing when the last one creaked. It had already been close to five hours since she'd taken a pain pill. Definitely time for a couple more. Another ice pack couldn't hurt, either, and she probably should take one of her over-the-counter sleeping pills.

She shone her flashlight into the trees, where she was most likely to find a troop of baboons or vervet monkeys, or a bush baby.

Nothing.

She yawned, clicked off her flashlight, then headed back up the stairs to her chalet. If she didn't get some sleep, she was going to regret it tomorrow. And tomorrow she wasn't going to let Mr. Cowboy get between her and her filming.

A missed flight, flat tire, chased by a rhino and the accident with the Jeep... And he thought she was the one with the string of bad luck?

Something rustled in the bushes to her left. Meghan paused. She retraced her way down the stairs. Eying the row of bushes, she backed up a couple steps, then slammed into something solid. And warm.

She spun around, her heart pounding as she wrenched her knee in the process.

"Ouch!"

"Meghan?"

The silhouette of Mr. Cowboy appeared out of nowhere.

"Alex? You scared me to death."

"I'm sorry."

A porcupine dashed into the bushes and out of sight.

"What was that?"

"A porcupine."

"It sounded bigger."

"It's harmless," she assured him. "For the most part, anyway. What I want to know is, what are you doing out here in the middle of the night?"

He flipped on his flashlight and shone it on the ground between them. She tried to read his expression in the shadows and caught a fleeting hint of surprise. Or maybe it was guilt.

"I heard a noise and came out here to investigate."

She didn't buy his excuse. "We're in the middle of nowhere, out in the Africa bush that is filled with nocturnal animals, and you had to investigate because you heard a noise?"

"I could ask you the same question. Why are *you* out here?"

She pressed her lips together, then frowned. He was throwing her off. She was tired and her leg hurt, and he…he exasperated her.

She could always send him back to the U.S. She'd tried to call her project leader, Karen Barns, on her cell phone before going to bed but hadn't been able to get through. She was definitely going to call again and find out why in the world they'd sent someone with little to no experience in either making a documentary or the African bush.

She was a documentary film producer, not a babysitter. If he couldn't carry his weight, she'd have no choice but to send him back on the next fight out of South Africa. Which at this point was sounding more and more like a good idea.

"Okay." She might as well confess. "I heard something I didn't recognize. And I was right. It was you."

"I knocked over one of the pots. I didn't mean to wake you."

She didn't bother to explain that he hadn't woken her. That she'd been lying awake the past hour thinking about how she needed to finish up the documentary. Thinking about how uncomfortable the recent string of accidents made her. Thinking about how Mr. Cowboy had swept into her life…

She shoved away that last thought. They might have more in common than she'd expected, but that didn't mean she was ready for Prince Charming to sweep in or that she'd even know what to do with him if he did. She wasn't built for relationships.

"I was having trouble sleeping, heard something tapping on my window, then a crash, and decided to see what it was." Now that she knew it was him, she wished she'd simply stayed inside. There was no physical danger out here for her to explore—just increased danger to her peace of mind.

Alex glanced down at her darkened knee in the shadows. "Is your leg bothering you?"

"It'll be fine. It's just understandably sore and, yes, it's keeping me awake."

"You need to get it—"

"Checked out? I know. I've heard that before. It's nothing, though. Really. Just a bit banged up in a lovely shade of rainbow."

He laughed, then clicked off his flashlight. Lightning illuminated the sky. A slight drizzle had started to fall, adding to the coolness of the night. She might be ready to laugh off the incident, but he wasn't. He'd promised her father to keep his real identity a secret, but clearly keeping Meghan in the dark regarding that identity wasn't going to be easy.

Because he couldn't watch her constantly, which left him unsure how to proceed. In the past when he'd been involved in guarding civilians, they had a safe house, full disclosure and backup. But this was a different situation. Meghan wasn't the suspect in some case he was investigating or the witness getting ready to testify. She was an innocent victim caught up in a battle that wasn't her fault. And she didn't even know what she was up against.

The only thing in his favor right now was the upped security across the reserve due to the poachers. Tomorrow he needed to brief Ian, the manager, about the situation and get to know the guards—

"Alex?"

He looked at her. Wind blew through her hair. Her eyes were bright, though her lips curled slightly downward. "Sorry, I was thinking."

He shifted his thoughts back to the matter at hand. Something was still bothering him. He needed more information. Needed to know what he was up against. Had someone been sent here to scare her, or was it only the poachers they had to worry about?

"Thinking about what?"

"About the poachers, for one. You said that the last person who got in the way of the poachers was murdered. What happened?"

She started up the path to her chalet, limp obvious. "You're worrying again."

He wanted to say it was his job. That while he'd love to be visiting his grandparents' farmhouse or even going out on safari every morning, as he would if this was a real holiday, his responsibilities ran far deeper than being an assistant producer of a conservation documentary. Doing his job without her knowing was going to be a challenge no matter how he looked at it. And first, he had to figure out exactly what he was up against.

"It didn't happen here," she said.

"Where?"

"Another reserve about a two-hour drive from here."

"And?"

"It was one of these situations when someone was in the wrong place at the wrong time."

"What happened?"

"One of the guards stumbled across the poachers as they were trying to leave the reserve. He was killed."

"Wow. I'm sorry."

"He was twenty-nine years old. Had a wife and a newborn baby. The poachers were after the rhino's horn—"

"I've heard people use the ground-up horn for medicine."

Meghan nodded. "It's primary market is Asia. Problem is, there's no medical proof that it does any good at all. Which means the guard was killed over a so-called medicine that doesn't even work."

"Did you know him?"

"No." Compassion was clear in her voice. "But several of the workers here did."

The rain was still holding off to nothing more than a few drops as the lightning flashed its purple tint against the open savanna, illuminating the acacia trees scattered across the landscape.

"It's a crazy, mixed-up world we live in," she said.

"Yes, it is."

Her gaze dipped as she shook her head. "Which is why I'm sorry."

Alex's brow narrowed. "For what?"

"For taking out my frustration on you. Sometimes living here is like being in the perfect world. Beautiful, secluded, sheltered. It becomes easy to forget the pain and suffering happening right outside the perimeter. But the poachers changed that, reminding all of us that we're vulnerable, even here. Today was another reminder of that, and I wasn't very fair in the way I reacted."

He was used to living outside the *perimeter*. He faced life-and-death situations on a daily basis, which was why sometimes he found himself forgetting there was actually any beauty left in the world.

Something brushed against his legs. Alex jumped back, jamming his calf into a thornbush. "Ouch."

Meghan laughed as she shone her flashlight on the intruder. "I'd say we found our nighttime visitor. Alex, meet Becky."

Becky snorted.

"Becky?"

Alex's first instinct was to run. He looked down at two hundred pounds of wild boar with the additional eight inches of protruding tusks. He'd seen a man impaled by one back home.

Meghan didn't seem concerned. "She's a warthog."

"I can see that, but is she…friendly?"

"Extremely. Tourists love her, and she loves the attention. And, if you ask me, I think she likes you."

Her laugh deepened as Becky rubbed her coarse hair against his leg. "I'm sorry, I shouldn't laugh, but the look of shock on your face…"

Meghan's laugh was contagious. He smiled. Here he was standing on the soil of his mother's homeland while a thunderstorm swept through, sharing a joke with a fat pig and a beautiful woman.

He laughed with her. "Why in the world is she called Becky?"

"Ian's daughter, Rebecca, named her and it stuck. She's quite legendary around here."

A flash of lightning caught her smile, warming him from the inside out. What was it about this woman that had him laughing over the antics of a favored pig? What bothered him even more was the strange feeling that her laughter was soothing the ache inside he hadn't even had time to sort out.

She cocked her head and caught his gaze. "Don't you have wild pigs on your ranch back in Texas?"

"Yes, but when I see them, I'm usually shooting at them and they're running in the opposite direction. My dad can make some mean barbecued ribs."

Becky ran off, her tail twitching straight up. "Now you've made her mad, talking about ribs and barbecues right in front of her."

Alex laughed again. "Thank you."

"For what?"

"It's just been a while since I've laughed like that."

She smiled up at him. "Me, too."

Maybe his father had been right. Alex hadn't planned on taking his vacation days at all in the near future, much less spending them on an assignment halfway around the world, but maybe getting away was the antidote he'd needed to keep from burning out.

But it wasn't just the crisp night air, or a friendly warthog named Becky, or the lightning striking in the distance across the savanna that gave him this feeling of lightness. It was the woman standing in front of him.

She sat down on the steps leading up to her chalet, making him hope she was as interested in prolonging the moment as he was.

"It is amazing here, isn't it?" Her question came out more like a statement. "Always changing, with so many layers of beauty."

"Yes, it's stunning."

He loved the way she didn't take what was around her for granted. How she appreciated the opportunity she'd been given to enjoy the small things. How she made him smile and laugh.

"Look out there. Straight ahead."

A line of elephants lumbered near the water hole, their bulky outlines looking like a gray pencil sketch across the horizon.

He sat down next to her, leaving a slight space between them. "I remember sitting out on the front stoop of my grandparents' farmhouse with them, my mother and my three sisters, watching a storm sweep across the bushveld."

How could a memory seem so far away yet close enough he could almost grasp it? He hadn't expected Africa to be the vehicle to dredge up so many forgotten feelings.

"Do you miss her?"

"Yes. I was twelve when she died, so most of my memories are hazy. I miss the impressions I remember of her. The smell of jasmine while standing with her in the rain. The diamond pendant she always wore around her neck. The color of her hair in the sunlight.

"My mother died when I was fourteen."

He picked up the tension in her voice. "I'm sorry."

"It was a long time ago, but you know what it's like to lose a parent."

"I don't think you ever completely get over it, no matter what happens."

The light of the night sky caught her frown, making him wonder if this was a subject better left untouched.

"Sometimes I think I've lost all of my good memories," she continued.

"They have to be in there somewhere."

He was trying to piece together what little he knew about her. Tragedy tended to either shatter or strengthen people. From what he'd seen, life had made her stronger. Smart. Funny. She knew how to laugh. Knew how to enjoy life.

"My most vivid memory is the Christmas she met a man at a party she attended for work. Donald Banks. I'll never forget his name. She had to choose between him and my father and me. In the end, she went with him."

"Maybe there were things that as a child you couldn't understand. Like the fact that she did love you."

"I guess I've always hoped it wasn't me—but it's hard to truly believe that. Even if I wasn't what drove her off, I wasn't reason enough for her to stay."

It gave them something in common. The void of growing up without a mother. The subtle longing for that missing maternal presence. He'd never admitted it to anyone, but he loved the mothering antics of his sisters. Who had Meghan had to fill that gap? Was it the reason there was so much distance between her and the father who clearly loved her?

"I suppose your sisters helped make up for your mother being gone?"

He smiled, pleasantly surprised that her thoughts had run along the same lines as his. "Oh, they still try to mother me with advice—especially when it comes to women."

Her laugh floated past him. He was surprised she was opening up, but there was something intoxicating about the jasmine-scented air and the darkness, making him forget that the woman sitting beside him was hardly more than a stranger. Perhaps it was having the same effect on her.

"How often do you get to see your sisters?"

He leaned his elbows against his thighs "We all try to make it to my family ranch several times a year."

"Tell me about them."

He couldn't help but wonder if she really wanted to know or if she simply didn't want to be alone.

"Julie's the oldest. She's married with three girls, ages six and under, and is a stay-at-home mom. Sara is a pediatric nurse and has two boys, five and seven, and a daughter who's fifteen. Camy is the baby—of the girls, anyway, as she's still three years older than I am. Single. A bit wild. Completely down-to-earth."

"Wow. Sounds like a wonderful, close-knit family."

"We are."

He heard the longing in her voice as she spoke and wondered what it was she was searching for. Family? Belonging? He knew firsthand from his own mother's death that the sense of loss could be difficult to recover from. How much worse must it be for Meghan? On top of the loss, she'd also had to deal with abandonment.

A drop of water splashed against his forehead. Another slid down his check. "The storm's moving in fast."

"Which is why if we don't get inside, we're both going to get caught in this downpour."

"I'll see you in the morning, then. Make sure you lock your door."

"I will." Lightning illuminated her figure as she stood. "And don't be late."

Alex headed toward his chalet with a smile on his lips. He'd come to Africa to take on a job with the sole purpose of protecting Meghan. What he hadn't expected was how much he'd enjoy her company.

Thunder rumbled above him, jolting his thoughts back to the present and reminding him why he was here. It didn't matter how enticing her company was—he'd paid once for getting too close to someone he shouldn't have, and he had no intention of making that same mistake again.

Meghan shut her chalet behind her, then locked the latch like she'd promised. If only she could lock away her thoughts that easily. No matter how deep she'd hidden her memories, their conversation had brought a scattering of them to the surface. Which left her feeling vulnerable...and fidgety.

She eyed her cell phone, her mind far too awake to sleep. Even if she had his number, talking with Alex further was definitely out. Her father would be asleep. She and Kate had become close over the past few months, but Kate would have gone to bed hours ago, as well. Kate had an estranged sister and understood the difficulties of family issues, but somehow, she knew that even if Kate was here right now, her mother wasn't something she was ready to talk about with anyone.

What had surprised her the most was the unexpected connection with Alex. After her mother's abandonment, trusting in love had become all but impossible, and as a result, she'd turned pushing men away into an art. All of which left her unsure as to why she felt so at ease with him. In the short time he'd been here, she'd already discovered his need to protect, along with the importance of family in his life.

And the fact that he was messing with her tranquility.

Meghan pulled open the top drawer in the nightstand and picked up the small box where she kept the locket her mother had given her on her fourteenth birthday—two months before she'd left. Four months before she'd died. It had taken Meghan a long time to accept the loss. After her family had fallen apart, she'd kept the locket as a reminder of what could have been. She'd always expected her mother to come back. For them to be a family again. But then the news of her mother's death had come, leaving Meghan to search for closure and forgiveness on a day-to-day basis.

She looked out the darkened windows, where the rain was beating against the panes. Alex had reminded her of all that, and she was letting her heart interfere with her head. Which was why she was going to do what she should have done before she went to bed. She grabbed her cell phone off her bed, pressed Karen's number, then began pacing the room, waiting for her contact with the film organization sponsoring the documentary to pick up. They were nine hours ahead of the West Coast, which meant while it was the middle of the night in South Africa, her friend would still be up.

She was about to hang up when Karen finally answered.

"Karen, hey...I hope I haven't caught you at a bad time."

"No, not at all. It's good to hear your voice. I was just talking to someone about you and wishing we could borrow some of your cool weather. This California heat feels hotter than the Sahara desert."

Meghan laughed. "Maybe you need to plan a visit here, then. It's cool and we've got a storm moving in right now."

"I'll take you up on the offer if I can ever find a few days off. How is the project going?"

"It's going well. We should be wrapping up most of the filming by the end of the month. Just waiting on Kibibi to introduce her cubs to the pride. I think the end product will be well worth the time and effort we've put into it."

"Good. I was worried there might be a problem when I saw your number pop up on my phone."

There wasn't a problem. At least she hoped not.

"I just have a question." Meghan hesitated. Maybe she was jumping the gun. "It's about Alex Markham. I was wondering where you found him."

"Alex…he was a last-minute hire, but he came highly recommended."

"For what?" Cattle rustler? Country line dancer? Heartbreaker? "The film industry—and wildlife, for that matter—doesn't seem to be his forte."

"That surprises me." Papers rustled in the background. "I had Clint handle his hiring, so I don't remember all of the specifics, but I did glance at his résumé. It was actually quite impressive. Has experience in tracking, photography, administration, and he owns a ranch in Texas. Funny, he almost sounds like a bona fide cowboy, if you ask me."

"That would describe him." Meghan frowned. Karen made it sound as if he was overqualified rather than underqualified. Which was why she shouldn't have called. Instead of giving him a chance, she'd let emotions skew her judgment. "It's not that he isn't capable—it's just that I was under the impression that he was…"

That he was what? He hadn't even been here twelve hours and she was ready to fire him because he'd made the mistake of getting between a mama rhino and her baby and was unnervingly good at getting under her skin. Which was why, if she were honest with herself, she'd have to admit she was actually calling Karen—because Mr. Cowboy had managed to dig through the protective wall around her emotions and stir up memories she wanted to avoid.

"You know, I'm sure he'll work out fine." Meghan tried to backpedal. "We only have a few weeks left, anyway."

"This late in the game, I don't see it feasible to replace him," Karen agreed. "Besides, the production assistant's role is critical, I know, but it doesn't take a brain surgeon to log video data and keep track of film footage."

"You're right." Meghan said. "I understand, of course."

"I know you're under a lot of pressure to get this finished, but I have no doubt of your and Kate's abilities."

A few minutes later, Meghan ended the call, wondering if she was really worried he wouldn't be able to do his job or worried that he made her heart feel again. Or maybe it was simply the string of accidents that had her feeling restless. While she still didn't believe there was anything to be concerned about, if someone was behind the accidents, Mr. Cowboy might end up being a useful man to have around after all.

FIVE

By the time Alex reached the main lodge the next morning, the Milky Way had just begun to fade into the gray-blue-tinted African sky. He figured while he might not be able to make up for yesterday's rhino fiasco, at least he could make a good impression and be on time like Meghan had ordered.

A row of yellow lanterns hung above the brick path, creating a warm glow despite the chilly morning temperature. A far different feel from his normal morning commute. City traffic, crime scenes and court dates had been transformed into a safari camp with thatched structures that seemed as if they came from another time or another world.

He drew in a deep breath, relishing the solitude. The only noise was the chatter of birds who'd been up before dawn. Meghan was right—it was amazingly beautiful here.

That almost made up for the fact that he was jet-lagged, freezing and exhausted after staying up half the night to ensure there were no surprise visitors to Meghan's chalet. He buttoned up the front of his denim jacket to block the chill and shoved his hands into his front pockets. This definitely wasn't turning out to be a very restful vacation. And the act he'd have to play only added to his stress. While he respected the wishes of her father, he was still worried that Meghan's not knowing what was going on would only end up putting her at further risk.

Which left him with one probing question. Should he follow her father's orders and leave her in the dark or let her know that she might be up against something more than just a handful of poachers? After spending half the night weighing the consequences of both actions, he still didn't have a clear answer. He simply didn't have enough information.

He walked to the edge of the parking lot, his breath fogging up the air in front of him. A group of Japanese tourists were arriving from their chalets, cameras in hand, their animated conversations interrupting the quiet of the moment. Bundled up like Eskimos with coats and blankets provided by the lodge, they climbed into one of the open Jeeps for their morning safari as their ranger answered their questions.

Alex rubbed his hands together to create some warmth. He'd read up on the family-owned lodge on the plane during the fight over and had been impressed with the long list of amenities the lodge offered. But beyond the luxury suites, world-class cuisine and access to fifty-thousand acres, he'd found himself impressed with the reserve's conservation efforts, which stretched beyond the moneymaking tourist destination. And while this benefit might not make its way into the tourism brochures on the lodge, he appreciated the upped security since the last poacher's attack. The night guards would make his job easier, which was why he planned to make friends with them to guarantee he was kept in the loop. Besides, sharing the work would remind him to treat this as just another job. Staying purely professional would be a challenge if he couldn't let Meghan know why he was really there, but he'd find a way to work with it.

He stifled a yawn. This time, he had no intentions of barging in as a knight in shining armor to save the day. He'd already tried that route...with Shannon. He'd learned his lesson when he hadn't been able to keep her safe.

He moved until he was standing against the railing that overlooked the veld beyond the lodge. The tawny color of the bush spread out to his left. Memories surged. He'd fallen for her. Hard and fast. And she'd felt the same way. Given time, he'd planned to ask her to marry him.

That was before the shooting. A year later, he'd finally accepted that Shannon was gone, but he could not accept the way he'd failed Shannon. Failed her family. Failed himself. It didn't matter that the committee had found him innocent of any negligence or that he knew it wasn't possible to save them all.

I know what You're thinking, Lord. I need to put the past where it belongs...in the past.

But sometimes, letting go and forgetting wasn't possible.

Losing Shannon had cost him his heart, something he never planned to go through again. Which was why he had to ignore whatever unexpected attraction had managed to surface yesterday with Meghan. He'd keep his word, ensure Meghan's safety until the election was over, then he'd be gone.

Meghan appeared from the lodge carrying two tall mugs. Her limp this morning was subtle and her long pants covered what he was sure was a nasty bruise on her knee. She fit the part of safari guide completely in her long-sleeved khaki shirt and fleece vest, lightweight cargo trousers, with her hair pulled back in a ponytail and topped with a wide-brimmed hat.

He shoved away any wandering thoughts and smiled. "Morning."

"A punctual assistant. I'm impressed."

She smiled back at him, clearly a morning person. He'd skipped breakfast, opting for an extra twenty minutes of sleep. Seeing the mugs of coffee she carried made him regret his decision. Tomorrow he'd have to rethink his routine, but the combination of jet lag, early rising and worry had thrown his schedule off completely.

Meghan handed him one of the cups. "I figured you might need a bit of a jolt to keep you awake this morning. Jet lag can be a killer."

His smile broadened. "You're a lifesaver."

"I wasn't sure what you liked."

He took a sip. On the sweet side with a swirl of milk. "It's perfect. I owe you one."

"Yes, you do. Starting now." Meagan handed him the clipboard she'd been carrying under her arm, then started toward one of the parked safari Jeeps. "Samuel won't be going with us this morning since the lodge is full and they need the extra drivers. Kate will be here in a few minutes to help film, but your job is to keep track of the footage. I'll be driving, but in case you get any crazy ideas of chasing down another rhino, another accident won't go over well with the manager."

"I think we're pretty safe to assume that isn't going to happen." He glanced at the clipboard, then hurried to catch up with her. "What about the other vehicle? Any news on it?"

"Samuel told me they're planning to tow the Jeep in as soon as it's light, so it will be a while before we find out what went wrong."

He'd already decided he was going to find a way to look at the vehicle himself. He might not be a mechanic, but he knew enough to recognize the indicators of sabotage.

Meghan glanced at her watch. "Kate's late as always. Should be here in couple of minutes."

He stopped beside her at one of the Jeeps, hating the fact that he felt at a disadvantage. He was used to being in control and chasing leads with the authority of his badge behind him. In charge of an assignment, not assisting with unfamiliar work. Stepping off that plane had thrust him into an entirely different world.

Alex glanced at the clipboard, wishing there was a way to avoid what he was about to say. But there wasn't. "Because of the rush nature of filling this job, I wasn't given any specifics on what I would be doing."

His excuse sounded lame. He couldn't fake knowing what he was doing, and even if he tried, it wouldn't take her long to find out he knew nothing about making a documentary. The problem was, he'd been so focused on getting here and evaluating her safety, he'd almost forgot he was here for a real job he'd have to perform to maintain his cover.

"Your main responsibility will be as my production assistant. Besides logging all video footage, we do a lot of social media you'll be involved in. Beyond that, *PA* is simply short for *gofer*." There was a hint of amusement in Meghan's expression. "You know, go for this... go for that."

He forced a smile. "Yeah. I get it. No explanation necessary." And no explanation offered on his part for what he'd really be doing—which was keeping an eye out for anyone who might try to target her with any more "accidents" or subject her to any more threats.

Meghan took a sip of her coffee, chuckling inside at his reaction. He might have experience in tracking and photography, but something in his expression told her he was used to being in charge. This was definitely going to be interesting.

"Good. For starters, then, you'll need to keep the log sheets. The form is there—you will need to keep it updated with all the key data like location, date, time, description of what was filmed, et cetera."

"Okay." He stared at the Excel sheet as if it was a piece of alien technology. What had he been told about the job? "Anything else I should know before we get going?"

"Yes." She couldn't help but smile. "I brought you coffee this morning, but—"

"I'm on my own after today?"

"I'm impressed. You catch on quick."

He took another sip of the coffee, then let out a long sigh. "So what's on the agenda today?"

"We need to find Kibibi, our mama lion, and her four cubs. In the next couple weeks, she will introduce the cubs to their father and the rest of the pride. It's the last piece of our footage we need before putting the documentary together."

"Sounds good."

"Yesterday, as you might recall, you scared our star away."

"Yeah, I remember."

Meghan noted his frown but didn't let it bother her. She wasn't going to let him live that one down.

Kate ambled up to them, coffee in one hand and a large duffel bag of equipment in the other, looking as if she'd just crawled out of bed. Which she probably had. Kate's typical morning routine was to set her alarm so she had just enough time to throw on some clothes and tie back her hair before grabbing coffee and a muffin in order to make it out to the Jeep.

"Sorry I'm late. My alarm didn't go off."

"Kate's always late and always arrives with an excuse," Meghan explained.

"I heard that." She climbed into the backseat. "At least I'm creative and, once I'm awake, completely amiable."

To Kate's credit, she was a great editor and fabulous photographer. It was just the combination of early-morning drives and cold temperatures that she clearly wished to avoid. This morning, she came bundled up in a knit hat, fuzzy scarf and dark fleece jacket as if she was bracing for a snowstorm.

After eight months of working together, Meghan knew it would take Kate at least another thirty minutes to completely wake up. By noon, the sun would be out full force, and she'd not only pare down to a T-shirt and shorts, but be talking up a storm.

"Morning, Kate," Alex offered.

Kate looked at Meghan, to Alex, then back to Meghan again and sighed. "Don't tell me Mr. Cowboy here is another perky morning person like yourself, Meghan."

Alex laughed. "Sorry to disappoint you, but yeah, I am. Back home on my father's ranch, getting up at this hour would be called sleeping in."

Meghan smiled at Alex's response. She shouldn't like him. He was too unsettling—and moreover, he clearly had no experience as an assistant producer, which meant he had no business being here. But for some reason, even after calling Karen, she'd still spent half the night lying in bed unable to sleep and the other half dreaming of those blue eyes of his. Which made no sense.

She tried to bury her mixed-up thoughts. "Let's get going. The sun will be up before we know it, and we need to find Kibibi while it's still early."

Meghan winced as she climbed up into the driver's seat, while Alex got in next to her. The swelling around her knee had gone down during the night, but it was still going to be sore for days and purple even longer.

"I still think you should get it checked out," Alex said. "Just to be on the safe side."

There he went again. Mr. Cowboy turned Mr. Protective. "All a doctor would do is tell me to ice it and take pain relievers." She shot him her best smile. "I'm already doing both."

He didn't look convinced.

"Storm keep you up last night, Kate?" Meghan asked.

"Nope." Kate settled in beside the pile of camera equipment and zipped up her coat to just under her chin, then pulled one of the extra blankets around her. "Fell asleep listening to my sound machine. With the ocean in the background, I almost feel like I'm sitting under the Florida sun."

Meghan started the Jeep while Alex stretched out his long legs beside her. She focused on the dirt road, avoiding his profile and reminding herself that she didn't have time for the complication.

"We'll follow the road back toward where Kibibi and her cubs were yesterday and try to get a signal off her collar."

"Do all your lions have collars?" he asked.

Meghan nodded. This was good. Talking about work

would help her mind stay focused. "Most of the adults have VHF collars."

"How do those differ from a GPS collar?"

She pointed to the hand receiver Kate was holding on to that was connected to a directional antenna. "There are advantages to both types. VHF are much cheaper. They're also accurate enough for our needs, and the batteries last about three years. The disadvantage is that we have to be in the field to find them as the range is only about two kilometers. This makes it harder to track an animal that is continually moving."

"What's the advantage of the GPS collars?"

"They allow data to be collected any time of day and can be accessed remotely, which means we don't have to be out in the field to know where they are. It also means we can end up with some amazing tracking results. But they're also much more expensive. And unfortunately, money is always a factor."

"So, I'm assuming brand-new GPS collars aren't in this year's budget."

Meghan shook her head. "Only for our rhinos. The radio pulse speeds up if the rhino starts running or lies down in the same position for too long. Of course, if you really want to go high-tech, satellite collars are the most effective way to collect current data on the animals' location, but while the data is always available, the price tag that goes with them makes them even more unobtainable. Especially with all the extra resources Ian has had to put into the security of the rhinos."

"Take the dirt road to the right, Meghan," Kate said from the backseat. "Looks like Kibibi's a kilometer or so past the water hole."

Meghan turned off the tar road onto another bumpy dirt road. Thirty seconds later, she pressed on the brakes as a family of elephants emerged from the bush and began filing across the road in front of them.

She started snapping photos, capturing their thick, wrinkled gray skin, long white tusks and wide flappy ears, then paused to catch Alex's expression. Mr. Cowboy clearly hadn't been this close to an elephant before. Or at least not one outside of a zoo. He sat forward, eyes wide open, jaw dropped.

She smiled at his awe, glad that she could share this moment with him and yet wishing he wasn't so ridiculously good-looking. Wishing he didn't stir up emotions she preferred left buried. "What do you think?"

"That we're at least a dozen yards too close for my comfort." His hand gripped the side of the Jeep. "It's not as if I've never seen an elephant, but up close like this…they're ginormous."

She laughed. "Besides that?"

"Seriously, I was impressed watching them from a distance, but this…this is incredible. The way they fan their ears, harbor those babies beside them…and those trunks!"

She was enjoying his reaction. Too much. He was right, though. There was something incredible in watching those mamas, sisters, aunts and babies plod past with their trunks swaying in front of them. A moment later, they'd completely vanished back into the sparse winter brush.

"We're almost to the water hole. We'll stop there for a few minutes to give you a bit of a taste of an African safari, then track down Kibibi."

The sun was just beginning to make its first splash of color against the horizon when Meghan pulled the Jeep alongside the water hole. Alex stared at the assortment of giraffes, impalas and warthogs as a male elephant lumbered up to take his morning bath.

Here the terrain seemed wild and untouched. Tall beefy tree trunks, flat leafy tops, a scattering of thorny bushes and desertlike flowers in an array of oranges, yellows and reds stretched as far as he could see.

The giraffe spread its legs at the water's edge and bent over to drink. This was what he'd hoped to experience. The heart of South Africa. His mother's homeland. To revisit where she'd lived, eat the food she'd loved, experience the people and land she'd called her own. This was why he'd agreed to play babysitter for Ambassador Jordan's daughter.

He'd expected to be moved. What he hadn't expected was to feel so overwhelmed by it all. Surrounded by God's majesty, he remembered what Meghan had said the previous night, about how far away this world seemed from any pain or suffering or crime.

He'd have to remember that was just an illusion. Crime could intrude anywhere—and would, if he didn't remember to stay on his guard.

A group of reddish-brown impalas, with their white bellies, startled, then bounded away from the water's edge into the bush.

He heard the click of Meghan's camera beside him. It pulled him from his thoughts—and a place he didn't want to revisit. He looked at the woman beside him, still unsure why he felt so comfortable with her. In the little time he'd known her, he'd found her dedicated, focused, charming…everything he looked for in a woman. If he was looking, which he wasn't.

She shut off the motor, letting the quiet of the morning spread out in front of them. A dozen elephants made their way to the water's edge, the younger ones trying to keep up with their broad steps.

"I'm guessing this is the same herd of elephants we saw a few minutes ago?"

Meghan nodded. "Ella is the matriarch. You can recognize her by the scar on the left side of her belly."

"She's beautiful. Except for infrequent visits to my father's ranch, I think this is the closest I've come to solitude in months."

"I could sit out here for hours just waiting and watching. There's always something new to capture on film."

Meghan snapped photos of the sun rising behind them while Kate filmed from the backseat. He was content just to sit and watch.

"When you visited South Africa with your mother, did you ever get to see something like this?"

Alex shook his head. "I went hunting with my grandfather a couple times, but never on an organized safari. As far as wildlife, all I remember seeing is the backsides of warthogs and a few baboons trying to steal my grandmother's produce."

Meghan laughed. "Do you like photography?"

"Yes, I…" He started to answer, then stopped. Photography was part of his work, in a way he couldn't discuss with her without unveiling the truth. He'd photographed dozens of crime scenes and taken miles of surveillance footage, but those scenes were a world away from the beauty of the African savanna. And the woman sitting beside him.

"Try this camera," she said. "The lens is heavy, but you don't need a tripod, which for me is a huge plus."

Her fingers brushed against his as she handed him the camera, causing the hairs on his arm to stand up. He tried to interpret a reaction that didn't make sense.

Somehow Meghan Jordon had managed to capture his attention. Completely. Which wasn't supposed to happen.

"Don't worry." Meghan took his hesitation as inexperience. "You can't break it. It's built like a tank."

"I was just—" He gripped the foot-long lens, wishing he could explain. But both his crime-scene experience and his tumultuous reactions to her were off-limits topics.

He zoomed in on the baby elephant hovering beside his mother's round, gray belly for protection and clicked. The baby splashed, its tail flapping away the flies, ears fanning back and forth in the morning breeze. One of the adults picked up tufts of grass along the water's edge. Focused on the animals, his nerves began to calm.

"Meghan, we're getting a signal for one of our lions."

Alex glanced back at Kate, who was holding up the handheld receiver with its antenna. He'd almost forgotten she was in the vehicle with them.

"Kibibi?" Meghan asked.

"No, Tali."

Meghan drove away from the water hole, in search of the other lioness. Five minutes later she caught sight of the tawny female.

"There she is." Meghan pressed lightly on the brake. "They're not off on a morning stroll, Kate. They're after an impala."

Alex held up the camera. "What do you want me to do?"

"Keep shooting. I'm going to get us closer."

Alex zoomed in on the lioness and kept clicking still shots. Maybe he'd been wrong about there being nothing but peacefulness and tranquility in this scene. The lioness deftly separated the impala from the rest of the herd. Shoulders hunched, body low to the ground, she moved forward slowly. A second lioness crouched on the left. The impala kicked his hind legs and tried to leap toward safety, but it was too late.

Alex balanced the heavy lens and kept taking photos as both lionesses lunged after their prey, then felt a moment of hesitation. The danger of the kill wasn't the only thing he sensed. The smell of cigarettes lingered in the air.

SIX

Tires crunched against gravel as Meghan pressed her foot on the accelerator and eased the Jeep forward. Her heart beat as fast as the fated impala's. The lioness snatched the impala's neck in her jaws and pulled the dying animal to the ground.

A moment later the attack ended.

This morning's kill wasn't the first time she'd witnessed the darker side of life in the bush. That thin thread dangling between life and death across the African plain was complex. She'd documented everything from the miracle of birth to the terror of the kill. They were each elements in the circle of life that couldn't be ignored.

While the impala lay still on the ground, the females walked away and the male lions took over. Alex snapped another dozen shots before handing her the camera. She paused before looking at them, wondering if she'd made the right decision to have him shoot the scene.

Photographing a kill was rare. Photographing the scene in perfect clarity even rarer. If she were lucky, one or two of his photos would be usable. Anyone could click the button, but handling a 400 mm lens took time to get used to.

She viewed the first photo and sucked in her breath in surprise. Instead of the blurry, amateurish photos she'd expected, he'd caught the details at close range. The lioness was vividly portrayed crouched forward, watching her prey. Eyes focused, shoulders raised as she crept closer. The muscles in her legs visibly rippled beneath her tawny coat.

"Are they okay?" Alex drummed his fingers against the armrest between them.

"Okay? Yeah. They're better than okay. These will be stunning for our next blog post." She continued flipping through the photos on the view screen.

A few of the shots were out of focus, but the majority captured the progression of the lionesses' stalk in incredible detail. Yellow grass framed the female's face sitting hunched in the shadows for protection as she waited for the perfect moment to strike.

"I'm impressed. Very impressed." She shook her head. "We should have hired you as an extra cameraman instead of a gofer with these hidden talents."

He laughed, and she caught the hint of relief in his eyes. "I'm not sure I'd go that far, but I'm glad you might be able to use them."

"You've clearly had some experience." Her words came out as a statement rather than a question.

His focus switched for a moment to the male lions continuing their feasting before responding. "I've always had an interest in photography. Took some classes at a local community college, mainly for my own personal use. I've never had a chance to test my abilities in the open bush like today."

"I find that hard to believe." She held up the camera, focused the lens, then shot another sequence of photos.

"There's a learning curve when using a longer lens. Beside that, not everyone has an eye for composition."

Something Mr. Cowboy definitely had.

"My mother was an artist, though I can't claim to have inherited any of her talents. If you like these photos, you should know that they're about as good as you'll get out of me when it comes to anything artistic."

Despite the modesty of his response, Meghan was beginning to think that Karen was right and that she'd rushed to judgment. Mr. Cowboy was apparently more qualified than she'd first given him credit. Despite his initial fumbles on arriving, he might actually turn out to be an asset if he could keep up with paperwork as well as he could film female lions honing in on their breakfast.

She kept snapping photos, wishing the man sitting beside her didn't fascinate her as much as the scene she was photographing. Beneath his cowboy veneer was a depth she found herself wanting to explore. A depth entangled with a hint of mystery that was managing to keep her off balance.

"What kind of artist was your mother?"

"Oil paintings mainly. Nature scenes. Some wildlife. My father has a number of them hanging up at the ranch."

"Which reminds me of something. I spoke to my boss last night on the phone." She turned to him and caught his gaze. She wasn't going to mention how his overprotectiveness had her looking over her shoulder constantly or that his nearness had her heart pounding, but she still had some hesitations about him. "She happened to mention to me that you own that ranch."

So she'd been checking up on him. Alex had expected the personal questions to start at some point,

but it still took him by surprise. What else had she un-
covered? Did she know that he was a Ranger? While
he intended to respect the request of her father if at all
possible in keeping his real reason for joining her production team a secret, he'd prefer not to have to flat-out
lie to her. Working undercover had always stretched his
comfort zone. He'd learned early on that the closer he
kept to the truth, the easier it was. A string of lies typically brought nothing but trouble.

But that didn't mean she had to know everything
about him, either.

"It's a fourth-generation family ranch called La Bella
Raina, named after my great-grandmother."

Her eyes widened as she nodded toward his hat. "So
you really are a cowboy."

"You could say being a cowboy's in my blood."

She flashed him a broad smile. What was it with
women and cowboys and cowboy hats? He looked away.
What was it with him and safari girls? Or rather, one
particular girl. Of course, what interested him in the
woman beside him went a whole lot deeper than her
khaki safari jacket and hat.

"Tell me about the ranch."

Alex hesitated. As long as he could keep the conversation focused on West Texas, he should be safe. At
least, that was what he was hoping. "It's still a working
ranch. My great-grandfather drove two thousand longhorns down from Colorado back in the late eighteen
hundreds. Built a bunch of corrals and a homestead,
then over the years expanded from there."

"Wow. I've never been to West Texas, but I bet it's
beautiful."

"It reminds me of South Africa in a lot of ways.

Rugged with small mountain ranges. Acre upon acre of bush, cactus and wide blue skies."

Meghan set down her camera for a moment. "So, I have to ask. Why apply for a job as a gofer? Isn't it a bit of a demotion from ranch owner?"

"I needed a change of scenery, knew the job was temporary. It seemed perfect."

A perfect distraction, anyway. She didn't have to know he spent most of his time away from the ranch, canvassing neighborhoods, running interrogations, gathering evidence and photographing crime scenes. And she definitely didn't need to know about the woman he'd failed to protect—the woman he'd buried his heart with a year ago.

"But wouldn't a vacation have been an easier route? Especially if you wanted to see your mother's home."

"I—"

"Kibibi's moving again, Meghan."

Kate spoke up from the backseat. He'd almost forgotten she was in the vehicle with them. As a person who paid attention to details, he was surprised Meghan had managed to completely distract him. Which was a major problem. He was here to keep her out of danger. Period. And he couldn't do that if he let his attention stray.

Meghan snapped a few more photos as the females moved closer to the kill. "They won't be going anywhere for a while, though I would like a few more shots from a different angle." She signaled to Kate. "We need to go around to the other side of that crop of bushes for some close-up video."

"Closer than this?" Alex asked.

At the moment, stepping out of the vehicle with a pride of hungry lions in the vicinity didn't seem like the best way to ensure she stayed protected.

"You're actually thinking about getting out of the vehicle?" Alex brushed her arm with his fingers, then pulled back. The idea seemed crazy. How was he supposed to guard someone who didn't seem to possess an ounce of fear over an animal who had just ripped an impala in two? He might not be an expert, but he knew enough about the bush to recognize the dangers. Forget the threats made against her—this was simply foolishness. "You can't go out there on foot."

"I can't?" Her eyes widened, but there was a hint of amusement in them. "This isn't the pride where the male lion has the final say, especially when I'm the boss here. Besides, you worry far too much."

"I'm just being smart. Without any kind of weapon for protection—"

Her raised eyebrow dismissed him. "We'll be fine."

Alex frowned. He could see he was annoying her with his overprotectiveness. Clearly she knew the risks. And knew they were all risks she was willing to take to get the footage she needed.

He wasn't sure what approach to take to change her mind. "This isn't the zoo with a fence. This is the wild where there are no boundaries or fences or safety zones."

"If it will make you feel better, keep the motor running just in case we need to make a quick getaway."

Her smile might make his knees feel week, but he wasn't buying the backup plan.

In the background, the male lions roared as they tore apart the impala. If she asked him—which she wouldn't do—this was nothing more than a recipe for disaster.

She grabbed her camera back and opened the Jeep door, then looked back at him. "They'll fill their bellies, then spend the rest of the day lounging. They won't even notice we're here. I promise we won't get close enough for them to bother us."

He nodded. "And I'll be right here waiting to sweep in and save the day when those lions decide they need dessert."

His response made Meghan laugh as she jumped out of the Jeep, camera in hand, trying to ignore the pain in her leg *and* the fact that he was concerned about her. Maybe what was really bothering her was that she liked having someone worry about her. Which sounded crazy. Her father had always been uptight, but his worry had never truly been directed toward her. Or rather, he'd never seemed afraid that she'd get hurt. Mostly it appeared that he expected her to disappoint or embarrass him, say the wrong thing in front of his colleagues. He was anxious she'd be late for a meeting. Never really worried about her and her needs. That was something for the boarding school to take care of.

Still, it was oddly reassuring to know someone was looking after her, even if she didn't really understand why he seemed so protective.

Kate crouched down beside her a safe distance away from the feast. The females had finally been given permission by the males to join in. She held up the camera and started filming, her focus on the scene in front of her not keeping her from teasing Meghan. "Have you noticed you've been acting like a schoolgirl all morning with a Texas-size crush?"

Meghan pulled back her camera and stared at her friend. "A Texas-size crush? Are you serious?"

"'You've got some talent'…'we should have hired you as an extra cameraman'…'you really are a cowboy.'"

Meghan felt her face flush as Kate mimicked her

comments in the Jeep. She turned back to the lions devouring their kill. She'd only been trying to be nice. Throw out a few deserved compliments as she got to know him—on a professional level only. Nothing more. Because she had no interest in Alex Markham in *that* way. Just because she couldn't help her reaction to his good looks... Well, she was human.

"So I let him use my camera and he took a few good—great—photos that I complimented him on. I find the fact that he owns a ranch interesting, but that doesn't equal a crush of any size."

"You've been flirting with him ever since he arrived. And back there in the Jeep, you completely forgot I was even there."

"You're wrong on both counts. I was definitely not flirting." Meghan lowered her camera. She enjoyed working with Kate, but today something had robbed her of all common sense. "I'm trying to be nice. Nothing more."

Kate raised her eyebrow. "I don't remember your being so nice to Jared."

"Jared was...Jared."

Meghan frowned. Okay. So there was a slight difference. Jared was a twenty-two-year-old intern. He was nice. Even good-looking. And as for his work ethic, he'd been reliable and dependable.

But he didn't make her heart stir.

Not that Alex did, either, of course. She took another peek at the Jeep. Apparently Mr. Cowboy had forgotten about the dangers of her stepping outside the relative safety of the Jeep and was enthralled by watching the pride.

He was good-looking. Okay, better than good-looking. He sat in the Jeep, cowboy hat tipped back, perfect-fitting black Wrangler jeans and boots. He looked as if he'd be just as comfortable working a tractor as sitting on the back of a stallion. She could picture him out on that Texas ranch, feeding livestock, mending fences, moving herds and hauling hay with the deep colors of the sunset behind him at the end of the day. Most of the guys she knew back home rarely stepped out of their cubicles and away from their computer screens. They were definitely not the outdoor type. Definitely not the cowboy type. And definitely not her type.

Not that she was looking for the cowboy type. She wasn't. Just like she definitely hadn't been flirting.

"See what I mean?" Kate interrupted her thoughts. "You can't keep your eyes off him."

"I was just—" *Daydreaming. Ugh.* She hated getting caught. But that didn't mean she was going to admit it. Not yet, anyway. "You're imagining things."

"Am I?"

Meghan pressed her lips together. She shouldn't be defending herself, because this wasn't some junior-high feud. Still… "He took some great photos. Is he good-looking? Yes. Interesting? Yes. But I'll say it one last time. That doesn't mean I was or am flirting with him."

"The lady doth protest too much, methinks." Kate kept her camera going as two vultures set down a dozen feet away, waiting for their turn with the kill. "Jared knew his job, did everything you asked him to without ever complaining or questioning. Alex, on the other hand, clearly has taken your heart and turned it upside down."

"My heart has yet to move in any direction."

"Then tell me what happened after the rhino charging last night that left you stranded out there together."

Meghan rolled her eyes at Kate. "We talked. We connected over a few things we have in common. He lost his mother like I did. She was from South Africa, so he has a love of this country."

Kate pressed her lips together, looking apologetic. She knew that Meghan didn't find it easy to talk about her family. "You know I'm just teasing. Besides, you don't have to make excuses on my account." She focused on the view screen of the camera. "Personally, I can't say that I blame you. If I wasn't still reeling from my last broken relationship, I might be giving him a second look."

"Trust me, Kate. You can have him."

"I don't think it matters what I think—our Mr. Cowboy clearly only has eyes for you. I've seen the way he looks at you."

Meghan set the camera down and turned to her friend.

"The way he looks at me?"

Now Kate was being just plain crazy. Meghan had known Alex for less than twenty-four hours. They'd be done here in another couple weeks. After that, he'd go back to doing...whatever a cowboy like him had done before he'd flown halfway around the world to play gofer for her.

"Finding yourself attracted to someone isn't the worst thing that can happen, you know."

"I never said I was attracted."

She never said she wasn't, either. But while Meghan might admit to an initial interest—honestly, who could resist a good-looking cowboy—that didn't mean she planned to act on it.

"What really has you running?"

"Running?" Kate's question caught her off guard. "Who said I'm running?"

"Come on, Meghan. We've spent a lot of time together over the past months in the bush, with nothing much to do beyond filming, editing and talking. This isn't the first time we've bared our souls about men."

Meghan nodded. "You know you're like the sister I never had, but Mr. Cowboy...Alex...is—"

"Different?"

"Yes."

"So why does that scare you?"

Meghan stared out across the water hole, not sure she wanted to go there. "What do I know about how to make a relationship work? When I look at my father, I see a man who placed his career over family and friends. That's not what I'm looking for."

"What are you looking for?" Kate asked.

"Someone who puts God first, sees family as a priority and is up for a bit of adventure."

Someone who made her feel worthy of being loved. Someone who could make her believe she was worth staying for.

"But it's not just a question of finding someone like that," Meghan continued. "Even if I met him, what guarantee would I have that he'd want me or that we could make a relationship work long-term?"

"So you're afraid and have a hard time trusting your heart—and common sense—to make the right decision."

"I suppose that's a good way to put it. I'll admit I find him interesting, fun, but—"

"But what? You're afraid?"

"Of course not."

"Admit it, who isn't afraid on some level? Afraid of getting hurt, of choosing the wrong person to spend the rest of your life with, afraid of making the same mistakes as your parents. Your past might play into the situation, but you'll never know until you try."

Meghan frowned. The girl was making far too much sense.

"Listen." Apparently Kate wasn't finished throwing out her advice. "Compared to most people, my parents have a perfect marriage. Thirty-five years this September. They do everything right. Work out their differences, don't go to bed angry, spend time together—they even still go out on dates. But in the end, their marriage isn't perfect, and while it's helped me believe that couples really can be truly happy together, I still have some of the same fears you do. Fears of rejection and loneliness."

"What are you trying to say?"

"Don't walk away—or run away, for that matter—because of fear."

Meghan steadied her lens and took a few more shots before slipping on the lens cap. "I don't even know him."

"I'm not talking specifically about Mr. Lone Star. Just remember when you find the right guy, it never hurts to give love a chance."

"Enough about my love life." Meghan stood up and brushed off her pants. "I need to grab the memory cards from the trail cameras, then we'll go find Kibibi."

She climbed up into the Jeep ahead of Kate, thankful Alex hadn't heard the awkward exchange. A Texas-size crush. Seriously, the girl had been reading one too many romance novels.

With Kate and the equipment back inside the vehicle, Meghan put the Jeep in Reverse, then headed back down the road toward the first camera. But trying to focus on anything but Mr. Cowboy's profile beside her was proving difficult. "I need to switch out the memory card on one of our trail cameras up ahead, then we'll track down Kibibi."

"How many cameras do you have set up?" He pulled off his hat, fiddled with the rim, then put it back on again.

"About a dozen throughout the reserve." She could do this. Talk about work. Nothing that could be misinterpreted as flirting. Nothing personal. "They're an additional way for us to track the movements of both predators and prey in this area."

"And poachers?"

"It wouldn't be the first time they've been caught using cameras like this. Our cameras have a no-glow feature as an extra security measure for that very purpose."

Meghan turned down a bumpy dirt road that led to another smaller water hole, then stopped in front of a group of tall, spindly trees. Grabbing an empty memory card from her camera bag, she eased out of the vehicle and headed for the edge of the grove. The process was simple. All she had to do was switch the cards, take the old one back to the lodge and see what they'd captured.

She stopped in front of one of the trees and frowned. The camera was gone. She looked down the row of trees but knew she was in the right location. She'd visited this spot a couple dozen times over the past few months.

"What's wrong?" Kate called out from the Jeep.

Meghan turned back, irritated. "The camera's gone."

"What do you mean, gone?"

"I mean it's gone. Vanished."

Meghan turned around too sharply and felt a blast of pain shoot up her leg. "Are we in the right spot?"

Kate reached for the GPS in the front seat, then

jumped out of the Jeep. "Unless you inputted the information wrong—which we both know you didn't—it should be right here."

"I know."

"So what do you think? Elephants or hyenas?"

"Could have been either."

They both stared at the tree. It wouldn't be the first time a camera had been stolen or destroyed, but it was strange that this one had completely disappeared. Animals weren't usually that thorough. She started searching the brush around the tree for any signs of the metal case or camouflaged straps, trying to ignore the nagging thought in the back of her mind that this time an animal wasn't responsible. Alex was rubbing off on her with his aversion to the word *coincidence*.

"What are you thinking?" Kate asked.

She leaned over and rubbed the side of her knee. It was time for another round of pain medicine. "I'm thinking that Ian's going to start charging me for any more property damage."

"It's not exactly your fault."

"No, but I'm the one who convinced him that the cameras would be beneficial not only with the conservation program, but also as an antipoaching method."

Alex stepped up to the tree beside them. "Has this ever happened before?"

"You'd be surprised how often it occurs. Between curious animals, bugs and heavy rain, we've had our share of destroyed cameras. I was hoping the new straps we installed would make a difference, but apparently they didn't."

"But this time you don't think it is the work of a hyena."

She looked up and caught his gaze, trying to shake

the eerie feeling that they were being watched. "I didn't say that."

But she'd thought it. Meghan frowned. Mr. Cowboy and his ever-suspicious ways were definitely rubbing off on her.

"You're thinking poachers," she said.

"I didn't mention it, but I smelled cigarettes earlier."

She'd noticed the distinctive scent as well, but hadn't wanted to consider that angle. They'd found the cigarettes a half mile from here, which meant they could be nearby. Without the cameras, any possible evidence showing what the poachers were up to had been erased.

SEVEN

Alex studied the tree, trying to evaluate the evidence—or rather the lack of evidence. All they knew for certain was that the trail camera, once attached to the spindly tree in front of him, was missing. He'd hung his fair share of trail cameras and found that the majority went missing due to theft from humans. Not animals. Which made him lean to the conclusion that the missing camera was the work of someone who didn't want them to see what was on that memory card.

Alex turned to Meghan, tipping his hat slightly to block the sun that was finally up and trying to chase away the chill of the morning.

"You said this has happened before?"

"Yeah. We've had animals manage to pull them down on more than one occasion."

"Okay, then let's start there. I know what happens back in Texas, but what animal could have done this here?"

Meghan stared at the tree. "Elephants can be extremely destructive. We've discovered photos of their trunks as they ripped the camera off the tree. Baboons will wrestle the cameras from their cases and even a determined hyena can pull one down."

Alex ran his fingers down the rough bark. "And these marks?"

She shrugged a shoulder. "Could be a leopard. They leave claw marks on trees in order to warn other leopards to stay away. Samuel would be a better judge as to when these marks were made. What do you think, Kate?"

"I think Samuel definitely needs to look at this. I can shoot a roll of video, but forget tracking and reading markings."

Alex studied Meghan's expression and watched her frown deepen as she spoke. "You're right about the poachers. As much as I'd like to, we definitely can't rule them out."

The scenario did fit. Poachers came after one of the rhinos, realized they'd been caught on camera and destroyed the evidence.

"We need to look for the camera. When animals have managed to take one down, we've almost always found it. If we have the memory card, we should be able to see what happened and hopefully rule out the poachers."

"Just make sure you look both up and down while you're out here," he warned.

"Funny."

He caught her smile before they marked off a rough grid to divide the area and began searching. Finding a camouflaged camera in the thick brush was almost as bad as looking for a needle in a haystack.

Maybe he was making a big deal out of nothing, but Meghan was the one who'd brought up poachers. Poachers on the property meant danger, and he wasn't ready to take any chances with her safety.

He studied her from a distance. Intent. Determined. The sun caught highlights of red in her hair he hadn't noticed before. She'd made him laugh last night. Something he hadn't done for a long time. But getting involved emotionally in a case always led to trouble. And that was a place he wasn't going to visit again.

"You make sure you keep an eye out for Becky," she called out.

He shot her a wry grin. "Very funny."

Meghan laughed.

He turned back to his search. She was distracting him. Breaking all the rules of engagement he'd set and messing with his head.

Ten minutes later, he finished sweeping his section of the grid they'd marked off. "Anything?"

Meghan shook her head. "No."

"Me, neither," Kate said, walking up to them. "I don't think it's here."

Meghan moved to his side, hands against her hips.

"What do we do now?" Kate asked.

"If it wasn't for the poaching issues, I'd say we just chalk it up to another hyena or baboon. But if we're wrong and this is the work of poachers, Ian needs to know."

He nodded. They couldn't bank on coincidences. At least not at this point. He needed to figure out exactly what was going on. What threat might be from the poachers and what threats were aimed directly at Meghan.

Meghan pulled her keys out of her pants pocket and started for the Jeep. "I suggest we talk to Ian, tell him what happened. We can also bring Samuel out here to get his opinion. If he ends up finding evidence that one of the animals took it, we should be able to rule out poachers."

Fifteen minutes later, they were back at the lodge in

the reception area, where Meghan introduced Alex to Ian Clarke, a burly man wearing khaki shorts, a short-sleeved button-down shirt and heavy work boots.

"Ian, I'd like you to meet my new assistant. Alex Markham. Alex, Ian is the manager and part owner of the lodge and surrounding reserve."

Alex shook the older man's hand. "It's nice to meet you."

"Alex." Ian nodded. "Howzit?"

"I'm doing well, thank you."

"I'll admit I wasn't sure about this entire project Meghan's involved in, but my wife insisted that the exposure would be well worth any initial investment."

"And?"

"Turns out she was right. On top of the documentary, Meghan's blog about their encounters with the lions and other animals has received quite a following over the past few months. It's translated into upped business for the lodge."

Before he left Texas, Alex had read through her blog, where she posted snippets of her time with the lions through photos, video clips and essays on daily life in the bush. The woman was talented.

"Meghan told me she was getting a new assistant after Jared had to return home," Ian continued. "Sorry I missed your arrival. When did you get in?"

"Late yesterday afternoon."

"He was in the Jeep with me when the brakes went out," Meghan said.

"I'm just relieved neither of you was seriously hurt. I've got my mechanic fixing the problem right now."

"Was he able to determine why they went out?" Alex caught Ian's guarded reaction and immediately regretted asking the question. This wasn't an official agency case where he had jurisdiction to investigate.

"He means like sabotage, because he always jumps to the worst possible conclusion. You can ignore him, Ian. I've discovered he's a bit of a worrywart." Meghan shot Alex a smile. "And probably watches too many episodes of *Walker, Texas Ranger.*"

"Very funny," Alex said.

The woman was impossible. Cute, but impossible.

Alex tried to play down his question, hoping he hadn't just dug himself into a hole. "I'd just heard about the issues with poachers you've been having lately, and I thought it might be prudent to check all possibilities."

"You have a point, but even if poachers were somehow involved, there aren't really any measures I can take. We're in the middle of the bush. The local police department doesn't have time to get involved in a situation without proof of foul play, so there's not much I can do besides have my mechanic double-check for signs of sabotage." Ian leaned against the wooden counter and folded his arms across his chest. "Why do I have the feeling that the three of you aren't here just for introductions and questions about the vehicle brakes? Did something else happen?"

Meghan tucked her thumbs in the front belt loops of her pants. "One of the trail cameras is missing. I'm sure it's nothing more than a curious baboon at fault, but with the poaching and the issue with the brakes, we thought it was worth following up on."

"You're probably right." Ian frowned.

"Problem is, we can't find the camera, and without the memory chip, we're still in the dark as to who or what is responsible."

"What can I do to help?" Ian asked.

"We'd like to look at the tracking history of the rhinos over the past few days," Meghan said. "See if there was any activity near the camera since I last switched out the memory card. I think we also need to go out and check the other cameras, as well."

"I agree. With all that has happened, we can't afford to take chances and miss something. We can check the GPS tracking history in my office."

Five minutes later, Meghan pointed to the screen of Ian's computer. "Two nights ago, one of the rhinos was there."

Ian rubbed his beard. "And at the same time, our patrol saw an unauthorized vehicle in this area. They never found anything to confirm why they were here, but these poachers continue to stay one step ahead."

"So it's possible our poachers realized that they'd been caught on camera," Meghan added.

"Makes sense."

"I know he's busy," Meghan said, "but I'm going to see if I can get Samuel to come out there with us to check the other cameras before we head off to find Kibibi. Maybe he'll be able to spot something we couldn't."

Alex hesitated as the two women started to leave, then turned to Meghan. "Can you give me a few minutes?"

"Sure." Meghan pulled her sunglasses off her head. "I need to run to my chalet and grab some sunscreen. Meet us back out at the Jeep in fifteen."

Alex waited until Meghan and Kate left the office before turning back to Ian. "I was wondering if I could speak with you for a moment in private."

"Sure, let me just quickly give the mechanic a ring about those brakes."

While Ian spoke on the phone, Alex took a moment to study the rows of tourism awards along with the stunning prints hanging on the office walls. Two leopards in a tree. A cheetah nuzzling with her three cubs. Elephants drinking at the water hole. A close-up shot of a rhino with its magnificent horn. The man's résumé appeared to be as impressive as the photos.

Earlier today, he'd been almost willing to believe that the brakes—along with Meghan's recent run of misfortune—*was* simply a string of coincidences like she believed, but today's incident with the camera seemed to put things in a different light. Until he could find out exactly what was going on, he felt as if he was blindly attempting to protect her without knowing where the next attack was coming from. He needed to know more about the poachers in order to evaluate the threat against Meghan.

There was something, though, that made him hesitate at telling Ian the truth behind why he was here. Meghan had mentioned the effects of a downed economy on tourism and how poaching had become a new game that now included ranch owners, pilots, hunters and veterinarians in desperate need of a cash flow to make ends meet. Money was a powerful motivator, and the potential proceeds from the slaughtering of rhinos might easily prove to be enough to tempt even an honest man.

But Ian's reaction today to another threat seemed genuine. Reading people had become second nature over the years. Alex knew the physical signs: avoiding eye contact, fidgeting, blocking their mouth to cover up dishonesty. Ian had displayed none of these.

Alex shifted his gaze to the family photo on Ian's desk. Two boys and a girl, somewhere in the range between four and ten years old. Would he risk jail time and fines to ensure their financial stability?

He hoped not.

Ian set his cell on his desk. "My mechanic promised to double-check his work, but he says that it looks like the brake lines simply burst."

Alex nodded, hoping the man didn't think him paranoid with his questions. "Your photographs are beautiful."

"Thanks. My wife took most of them."

"She's definitely talented."

"She's won a few awards over the years, but I think she just likes being out there in the bush. She's visiting her sister in Cape Town with our kids at the moment, but she grew up on this reserve and spends a lot of time outdoors. She's been gone less than a week, and I'm sure she misses the bush more than she misses me."

Alex chuckled. "I don't blame her. It's beautiful here."

"She was the third generation to be born and raised here. We took over the day-to-day running of the reserve when my in-laws retired five years ago."

Alex's gaze shifted to a large family photo with the familiar thatched lodge in the background.

"Looks like a family affair."

Ian laughed. "It is. My brother-in-law lives in Johannesburg, working in accounting. He does all the books for the reserve. Here, with the help of a handful of cousins and second cousins, we deal with everything—food, employees, maintenance, marketing and the conservation project, not to mention the animals, employees and volunteers. The to-do list never ends when it comes to running a business like this."

"But you enjoy it?"

Ian sat down behind his desk and leaned back in his chair. "Despite the challenges, yes. Wouldn't have it any other way."

"Meghan's told me a little about the issues you and the other game reserves across the country have been facing with poachers."

"Men have been injured and even killed trying to stop them, not to mention the hundreds of rhinos they continue to slaughter." Ian shook his head. "It's a different world from what it was when my in-laws ran the reserve. Before 2008, there were on average a dozen rhinos poached every year. That number alone was tragic, but recently, those numbers have skyrocketed into the hundreds every year."

Alex sat down in the chair across the desk from Ian. "Who's behind the attacks?"

"Wildlife trafficking has become big money." Ian picked up a pen from his desk and started clicking the end. "With rhino horns worth more than heroin ounce for ounce, organized-crime syndicates have gotten involved. Police have arrested everyone from local game farmers to mercenaries to veterinarians, government officials and kingpins. It's all a game of profit."

"What kind of profit are we talking about?"

"Somewhere in the neighborhood of fifteen billion American dollars a year. Right behind drugs, guns and human trafficking."

Alex let out a low whistle. "And this is all to keep up the demand for some Asian medicinal practices?"

Ian dropped the pen back onto his desk and nodded. "Powdered rhino horn has become a status symbol for the rich. It's touted as a cure for cancer and a treatment for high fever—neither of which has been scientifically proven, despite many, many tests. They spice their drinks with rhino-horn powder believing it will make them more virile. Mixed with water or alcohol, it's used as a health boost or a cure for a hangover. I've even heard of it being given as an expensive gift or used as informal currency."

Alex shook his head. The whole idea seemed crazy.

"Little do they know," Ian continued, "that the rhino who produced the horn has typically been shot dead with an assault rifle by corrupt game-industry professionals and processed into powder by a crime syndicate. It's become an entire system of middlemen buyers, exporters and couriers that can get the horns from South Africa to Vietnam in less than twenty-four hours, and the demand just keeps rising, leading to more poaching. In another five years, if it isn't stopped, the rhino population will start shrinking until they are gone."

Alex leaned forward. He might not be here to deal with this issue, but the more he understood about the situation, the more he would know what he was up against when it came to keeping Meghan safe. "Is it just the rhinos they're after?"

"Lions are another hot commodity, as a collector's item rather than as a health aid. A complete skeleton can fetch up to ten thousand dollars."

"Wow. And what about your reserve? What kind of security have you implemented?"

"Everything I can manage financially. We've hired extra guards, bought GPS trackers for the rhinos, along with hidden cameras. We also try to stay under the radar and not broadcast how many rhinos we have. We check on them every day, tracking them by GPS. On top of that, we're in the process of ensuring all of our lodge staff receives antipoaching training. But there is only so much we can do. The crime syndicates supporting the poachers have deep pockets and can afford better resources than I can. So far we've lost two rhinos, and with the way things are going, they probably won't be the last."

"Meghan told me about the man who was killed on a nearby reserve."

"Did she tell you how?" Ian leaned forward. "The rhino carcass was booby-trapped with a hand grenade to scare off the response team. He died instantly. It was a wonder more weren't killed in the blast."

The entire issue seemed daunting. "My family owns a ranch back in Texas, but I have to say that our poaching problems aren't nearly as serious as the ones you're facing right now."

"I guess you documentary people are always full of questions. Looking at doing a documentary on the rhino crisis after this project?"

"No." Alex weighed his options. He hadn't planned to tell anyone who he was, but he needed inside information, which meant he was going to have to trust Ian. "There's something you need to know about me."

Ian's brow rose in question.

"The real reason I'm here," Alex continued, "has nothing to do with Meghan's documentary—or rhino poaching, for that matter. In fact, to be honest, I've never had experience with filming wildlife. I'm a Texas Ranger from the United States."

"A Texas Ranger?"

"I'm here unofficially as a favor to Meghan's father."

"I don't understand."

"Meghan's father is the U.S. Ambassador to Equatorial Guinea. There have been a number of threats made against his life and against his daughter in connection to the upcoming election."

"So he hired you to protect her?"

"Yes."

"What does Meghan think about this?"

"That's part of my issue." Alex hesitated. "Their relationship is a bit shaky, so her father doesn't want her to know."

"You haven't told her?"

"Until I know if the threats against her are viable, I'm respecting her father's wishes. But as you know, there have been a number of incidents surrounding Meghan lately."

Ian nodded. "Like the brakes going out on the Jeep."

"Exactly. Meghan insists that she's accident-prone, and maybe she's right that I'm a bit of a worrywart, but I need to see if we are looking at a specific threat against her that is tied to her father, a connection to the poachers who want her and her cameras out of their way, or if she really is just accident-prone and all of this is nothing more than a coincidence."

Ian let out a low laugh and folded his arms across his chest. "I realize that this is a serious issue, but if you ask me, I know Meghan, and you've got your hands full protecting her, whether she knows why you're doing it or not. She's spirited, independent and a real go-getter."

"Tell me about it." Alex felt some of the tension in his shoulders release. He'd done the right thing in talking with Ian. "I know her father has his reasons, but if I find her life is in danger, I will need to tell her. Which is why I felt I needed to talk to you."

"So you believe that the fallen hide and the brakes, for example, could be sabotage?"

"It's possible."

"Let's say they are some kind of threat against her. What would the point be?"

"That's what I need to find out, but a lot depends on who is responsible. It could simply be motivated by a determination to show her father that they are here and can get to her. He's being pressed to back the opposition in an upcoming election."

Maybe he was reading too much into this, but experience had told him to never to dismiss coincidences. More than likely, he was looking at two very separate situations. One, poachers doing what man had done for thousands of years. Two, viable threats against a man's daughter to manipulate the ambassador's actions.

But he also couldn't ignore the possible connection between the poaching and the upcoming election in Equatorial Guinea. If crime syndicates had started working with game-farm owners and vets, as Ian had implied, countries like Equatorial Guinea with lax policies on trafficking became a safe haven for those involved. He'd spent time reading up on the new regime trying to come to power—a regime with known ties to an international crime syndicate.

With the election looming, he needed to figure out how all of this fit together before danger struck again.

EIGHT

Six days later, Meghan leaned back against the raised seat of the open Jeep behind their driver while the crisp night air whipped through her fleece jacket. Above them hung the African sky, thousands of dots of light illuminating the familiar southern hemisphere with its arced Milky Way, famed Southern Cross and dozens of silvery nebulae and star clusters. With Kate battling a cold and needing to take some time off, tonight was the first time Meghan had gone out into the bush alone with Alex since his arrival—a situation that had her feeling both exhilarated and terrified.

Samuel drove them down the narrow trail, heading northwest toward where the transmitter had picked up Kibibi and her cubs. In the past week, they'd captured several more hours of footage of the family as they waited for Kibibi to introduce her babies to the pride. And while the week had thankfully passed with no more "coincidental" disasters or even any signs of poachers, she'd found herself continually struggling with the draw she felt toward the man now sitting beside her.

Which meant Kate hadn't stopped teasing Meghan, insisting she had a crush on Mr. Cowboy. But she'd yet to define her feelings. It wasn't just the fact that he was handsome, smart and had a Southern drawl that had her mesmerized. Instead it was his seeking faith, love of family and even his ridiculously overprotective stance toward her that had her wanting to take the time to delve deeper into what was behind that cowboy exterior. So far, she'd barely scratched the surface.

She snuck a glance at his profile. He still looked like a transplant from Texas with his denim jacket and cowboy hat, but after a week of shooting footage in the bush, he'd disproved her fears and proved to be both capable and hardworking. And while she might not be desperate for romance or even looking for a relationship, Alex had managed to awaken a piece of her heart she'd thought impossible to revive. He'd made her want to stop running. Made her feel safe.

A monkey hollered in the distance, in sync with the rest of the night's symphony pulsing around them with constant roars, chirps and whistles.

"So what do you think so far about your first night drive?" she asked.

The moonlight caught his smile. "It's incredible. I've seen animals on my father's ranch—wolves, deer, wild hogs—and of course I've watched the occasional African documentary on Animal Planet, but seeing the animals up close is different. And at night…this is like another world. A wild combination of fierce beauty and a rivaled fight for survival."

Samuel's spotlight caught a termite-eating aardvark— rarely seen in the daylight—skittering across the trail in front of them before vanishing into the thick bush. Alex's description was right. During the day, the animals tended to sleep. Night was completely different as the nocturnal animals took on the role of hunters in the cooler temperatures. Even the background music had changed from the constant chirping of birds to the haunting roars of the cats, whistling of insects and the occasional growl.

Samuel slowed down as the red-filtered headlights caught a rhino wallowing in the mud, casting a hint of color to the night's gray shadows.

"Why the red light?" Alex asked.

She searched the tree line for movement. "A bright, white light would startle them, but they don't react to the red."

A full moon hung above the conglomeration of stars, a subtle reminder of the afternoon he'd arrived when he'd tried to save her from the charging rhino. That night she'd introduced him to Becky, the warthog, and they'd ended up laughing in the rain. Had it only been a week ago that they'd first met?

"What made you decide to come to Africa?" he asked.

She turned back to him. His question surprised her. Except for that first night, most of their conversations had tended to edge away from the personal. "Not only did my father grow up in Africa, his work often brought him here, as well. But while he traveled extensively, most of the time I was stuck in some boarding school or living with my aunt in Southern California."

"So you never traveled with him?"

Meghan ignored the pang of regret wanting to surface. "He knew I loved traveling, so he did take me with him a couple times. Paris…Venice…Cairo. Each city completely captivated me. I knew that I wanted to do something one day that would allow me to see the world. Africa was always on the top of that list."

"Sounds as if you've been doing just that."

"When I graduated from college, my father connected me with a film company in the States and helped me get my first job as a production assistant."

"Which is short for *gofer,* I understand. Go for this—"

"Very funny." She laughed and felt her heart take a nosedive. "My first assignment didn't have the stunning backdrop of the bush. Instead, we were filming in Africa's largest urban slum in Nairobi. What about you? Your skill set seems petty diverse. Photography, ranching and my all-time favorite, paperwork. You've never really told me what you do for a living."

Alex hesitated with his response. It was the question he'd been expecting. For the past week, he'd managed to keep their conversations on the surface, enough to begin getting to know her without going too deep. Because as much as he wanted to learn everything there was about her, if he started asking personal questions, she'd do the same thing. It had been easy to keep things light with Kate in the vehicle with them. But something about tonight made him want to take a chance and delve deeper.

He stared out into the darkness, trying to form the answer he'd rehearsed a hundred times. He'd spoken to her father again last night. The wave of worry after the first couple days had subsided, making him wonder if the threats he'd received on her life had been nothing more than idle words meant to scare.

He still hadn't dismissed the connection between the poachers and the election, or the possibility that her string of bad luck was connected to those threats. But so far—including the crashed Jeep—he'd been unable to discover any tangible evidence of sabotage. And there was another issue behind the threats he had to consider.

Kill Meghan and there would be no leverage. Abduct her and the captors would face unwanted scrutiny. He assumed they'd want to avoid both.

He shifted his thoughts back to her question.

"Believe it or not," he began, "I graduated with a degree in finance. Had my sights on Wall Street."

"Wall Street?" He caught the surprise in her voice. "I'm not sure I can see you sitting in an office all day long."

"Turns out I couldn't. I spent three months in New York then headed back to Texas. Couldn't handle the pace."

Wind whipped through her hair and the moonlight caught her smile. "So what did you do from there?"

"Went back to work for my father on the family ranch."

He wanted to tell her he'd spent that first six months reevaluating his life. That eventually he'd decided to follow his uncle's footsteps and join the police force, a move that had ultimately changed his life. He'd discovered a deep-seated need to ensure justice prevailed, taking pride in ridding the world of those who preyed on the weak.

But he couldn't tell her any of that.

"Up ahead." Samuel pointed the spotlight into an opening in the bush. "To your right."

"Is it your lions?" Alex sucked in a breath, thankful for the distraction.

"Leopard." Meghan jutted her chin toward the animal, her video camera already going.

Alex caught the glint of the cat's eyes and started taking photos, hoping he could remember how to incorporate the tips she'd given him on shooting photos at night. His pulse raced. He hadn't expected the adrenaline rush the encounter produced. He hadn't expected that being here—with her—would affect him the way it was. Which was why, over the past week, he'd had to continually remind himself of the reason he was here. All he had to do was his job. Keep her safe until the election was over. Nothing more.

As moved as he was by the night air, the lure of his mother's homeland seeping through his veins, or simply the woman sitting beside him, this would be over soon. Elections would be held in another week. She'd be done filming a couple weeks after that. There was no reason for him to stay once his obligations had been fulfilled. And there would be no reason to ever see Meghan again.

The Jeep's headlights caught the muscular body of the leopard. Bulky, sleek, it walked within six feet of the Jeep, crossed in front of them with barely a glance in their direction.

A second later, it was gone.

Alex let the air out of his lungs. "I would have said it was a cheetah."

"Samuel's a better guide than I am, but the first difference is the spots, right, Samuel?"

Samuel nodded. "Leopards' spots are rosette-shaped, while cheetahs' markings are more round or oval. They also have tear lines that run from their eyes to their mouths. If you look at them side by side, you'll also see the leopards are bulkier, while cheetahs are lighter and taller."

"And the differences don't end with the physical characteristics," Meghan added. "Leopards hunt at night, while cheetahs hunt primarily during the day. Leopards are more solitary, climb trees and run a lot slower than cheetahs."

"I might have to watch my job." Samuel laughed. "You know as much as I do about these animals."

"I'd say you're safe, Samuel. You've got me beat by a long shot when it comes to tracking and actually finding the animals. In the end, that's what counts."

The tracker beeped on the seat between them. Meghan picked it up. "Kibibi seems to be moving. We need to head slightly more west, Samuel."

An eerie screech sounded behind them as they started moving again.

Alex looked behind him, but all he could see was blackness. "What was that?"

"Probably a baboon. They're known to scream when they don't get their way."

Something crashed through the bushes, then jumped onto the back of the Jeep. This time the scream was definitely human.

Alex shone his flashlight at the figure scrambling to get into the back of the Jeep. It was one of the guards. "Oscar?"

"They're after me! Please. Help me."

Gunfire ripped through the darkness, and a bullet hit the back of the Jeep.

"They've got weapons," Meghan shouted. "Hang on tight, Oscar. Samuel, get us out of here."

Samuel pressed the accelerator, and the Jeep roared down the trail. Brush whipped against the side of the truck as Oscar clung to the back of the Jeep. They might not be able to see who was behind them, but hopefully, they could outrun them.

Instinct took over as Alex handed his camera to Meghan. "I want you to get down and stay here. Turn off your flashlight. If they can't see us, they'll have a harder time hitting us."

A SERIES OF LOVE INSPIRED NOVELS!

GET 2 FREE BOOKS!

Plus, receive
TWO FREE BONUS GIFTS!

We'd like to send you two free books from the series
you are enjoying now. Your two books have a combined cover
price of over $10, but are yours to keep absolutely FREE! We'll
even send you two wonderful surprise gifts. You can't lose!

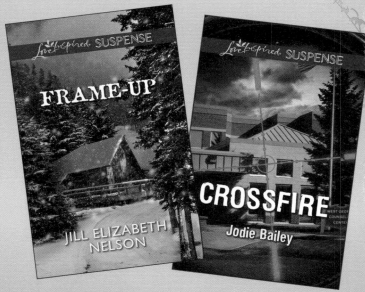

Each of your FREE books is filled with joy, faith and traditional values
and women open their hearts to each other and join together on a spiri
journey.

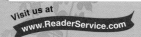

He climbed over the seat, careful to keep his head low. He might feel out of place working on a documentary, but facing an emergency head-on was how he was wired.

A second shot pinged off the back of the Jeep, then a third shot was fired. It sounded louder. Closer. Whoever was back there was gaining on them.

Alex gripped the metal side bar, trying to keep his balance as Samuel negotiated the rough terrain from the driver's seat. Grabbing one of Oscar's hands, Alex braced himself and attempted to pull him into the Jeep. Oscar lost his footing and slipped. Alex lunged for the man's shoulder, gripped his jacket and managed to drag him into the Jeep.

Oscar fell against the backseat, still gripping Alex's hand. "I think...I think I've been shot."

"Alex?" Meghan's voice was edged in panic.

"Hand me your flashlight and tell Samuel we need to get to the hospital as fast as possible."

He took the flashlight from her and, keeping the light beam low, searched for the wound. Blood soaked through his side. Oscar dropped his head back and groaned. Alex grabbed a blanket from the floorboard and pressed it against the wound. The Jeep bounced, forcing him to lose his grip.

Alex pressed harder. He wasn't sure how they were going to deal with whoever was chasing them, but from what he could see, if they didn't get Oscar to a hospital immediately they were going to lose him. Oscar cried out in pain, his eyes rolling back. Alex needed to keep him talking and awake.

"Tell me what happened out there, Oscar."

"They're going to kill me."

"Not if I have anything to say about." Alex checked the man's pulse. His heart was racing. "Who are they?"

"Poachers. They...they were carrying rifles."

"Did you see a rhino down?"

"No, but that doesn't mean they haven't already got to one of them."

Which meant that it might already be too late for the poachers' intended prey. But it didn't have to be too late for Oscar.

A bush smacked Alex in the face as Samuel headed for the reserve's front gate. Another shot rang out, sounding even closer than the last one. Someone else getting shot wasn't the only danger. With limited visibility it would be easy to badly damage the Jeep, leaving them out in the darkness with no way to get back to the lodge.

"What were you doing out there?"

"I...I was out making my rounds. They...they saw me and shot at me. I yelled and started running. I stumbled through the dark until I...until I saw your Jeep."

It sounded as if the poachers were trying to eliminate a witness.

There might not be an immediate connection to Meghan, but he still needed to know what they were up against.

"Could you identify them?'

The man was going into shock.

Alex shook him gently. "Oscar, could you identify them?"

He opened his eyes. "It was too dark to see them."

He knew that poachers had no qualms butchering the rhino, and often no qualms killing anyone who got in their way, either. Being the ambassador's daughter wasn't the only threat to Meghan's life at the moment.

Another shot ripped through the night, hitting the back of the Jeep.

"How far are we from the front gate?"

Megan turned around, still crouched low. They were surrounded by bush and few visible landmarks. "I don't know. Samuel…how far to the gate?"

"Five minutes." Samuel shifted the Jeep into a higher gear. "Another fifteen to the hospital if we hurry."

The moon peeked out from behind a string of gray clouds shedding narrow beams of light against the unpaved road. Blood was beginning to seep through the blanket. Alex pressed harder against the wound and started praying.

Meghan held up her phone in the hospital waiting room to check that she hadn't missed a call. Forty-five minutes ago, they'd arrived at the small rural hospital that served the surrounding towns and watched as Dr. Archer and a handful of medical personnel rushed Oscar toward the operating room.

Meghan stopped beside the window of the waiting room, quiet after a busy day of patients seeking treatment for everything from malaria to tuberculosis to HIV. At this late hour, the only other people in the waiting room, its walls covered in chipping blue paint, was an old man and couple with a child. The medical team hadn't told them what Oscar's chances of making it through surgery were, but Meghan hadn't missed the serious expressions on their faces as they'd whisked him away.

She turned to Alex, frustrated. "I left a message for Ian, but can't get him to pick up."

"Do you want to go into town and get something to eat while we wait?" Alex stood up from the cracked plastic chair he'd been dozing in and stretched his back. "I hear there's a pizza place that stays open late."

"I don't think I could eat anything." Poachers were back, a man had been shot and a rhino was possibly down. They'd planned to eat a late dinner after filming, but at the moment, eating wasn't exactly on the top of her to-do list.

"Maybe not." Alex glanced at the floor. "But pacing like this is only going to wear a hole in the tiles and there isn't anything we can do until Oscar gets out of surgery."

"I know, but—" Meghan's phone rang. *Finally.* "Ian?"

"I got your message about Oscar. How is he?"

"He's in surgery, so we don't know much yet, but it's serious. The bullet slammed through his side. The doctor said they wouldn't know what kind of damage had been done until they opened him up."

"You did the right thing taking him straight to the hospital."

"Dr. Archer said it was a decision that might have saved his life."

"Listen, I'm planning to come into town as soon as I can, but I'm waiting for the final reports on the rhinos."

"I understand." Finding another butchered animal would be a blow to the reserve that would be made even worse if Oscar died on the operating table. "There isn't anything you can do here right now, anyway. How many rhinos have you located?"

"So far all but two of the rhinos have been accounted for, but they found a cut in the fence where the poachers came in. We'll have to check again once it is daylight to see if it was the only one."

A moment later, Meghan hung up the phone, wondering if she should take Alex up on his offer of dinner. Samuel had gone to visit a friend in one of the wards, Ian wouldn't be here for a while and, in the meantime, Alex was right. There wasn't anything either of them could do but wait.

Meghan was about to say as much when the doctor walked into the room. She tried to read his tired expression, praying he had good news.

"How's Oscar?"

The doctor dropped his hands into the pockets of his scrubs. "The surgery went faster than we expected, but the bullet did a lot of damage, and he's still in critical condition. In fact, the only reason he is still alive is because you were able to slow the initial bleeding and get him here as fast as you did."

Meghan's hands clenched at her sides. Losing Oscar would be yet another senseless death. "Can we see him?"

The doctor shook his head, fatigue clear in the shadows beneath his eyes. "Not until tomorrow. We'll watch him closely during the night but know that, at this point, the odds are very low that he'll live."

NINE

Two police officers met them back at the lodge for questioning, looking to gain new information about the poachers. An hour after that, Alex stood beside Meghan in the lodge kitchen, heating water for the rooibos tea he remembered his mother drinking, hoping it would calm both their nerves. They'd missed dinner hours ago but, like Meghan, he wasn't particularly hungry.

The electric kettle clicked off, and he poured the hot water into the two mugs, then handed Meghan the pink polka-dot one. Her hands shook as she tried to take it from him.

"Whoa." He set the mug back down on the counter. "You okay?"

She looked up at him, her lashes laced with tears. "Yeah."

"No, you're not." He grasped her hands, which were trembling. "It's okay to be upset. Today was traumatic."

"I know." Meghan let him hold them for a moment before pulling away. "I can't stop shaking, and unfortunately it's not from the cold."

She dropped a tea bag into each of their mugs.

"Milk and sugar?" she asked.

She was changing the subject, but he didn't blame

her. She grabbed a canister from one of the shelves, clearly working hard to pull herself together.

"Have you ever eaten a rusk?"

He eyed the hard, rectangular-shaped biscuit. "I don't think so."

"Think biscotti with a South African twist. You dip them in your tea. I like them so much I've seriously thought about taking a suitcase full back to the States with me when this project is over."

He laughed with her, knowing she was searching for a way to cope. And wishing he could whisk her away somewhere safe where there were no poachers and no threats against her life.

Ian walked in from the dining room. Lines of fatigue were etched across his forehead. They weren't the only ones feeling the stress of today. "I know the two of you missed dinner. There's some homemade butternut soup and roasted chicken I can warm up if either of you are hungry, along with a couple slices of milk tart."

Meghan dipped a rusk into her tea. "This is all I want. Well…this and a good night's sleep."

Alex leaned against the counter and took a sip of his tea. He didn't want to sound like an interrogator, but he needed answers. "What did you find out there tonight?"

Ian helped himself to a slice of the cinnamon-dusted tart. "One of the rhinos had been darted in his side, but thankfully, Oscar's security team scared off the poachers before they were able to kill him or saw off the horn."

"What about Oscar's family?" Meghan asked. "Were you able to get ahold of them?"

Ian nodded. "I spoke to his wife. She's been visiting her mother for the week and will return tomorrow."

Alex nodded, praying that Oscar would make it

through the night to see his wife and daughter to-morrow.

Ian rubbed the back of his neck. "I'm frustrated be-cause we're not doing enough to stop them. Frustrated because one of my men was wounded—possibly fatally—tonight. Losing an animal is devastating, but to lose one of my men…"

"How do you stop them with the demand—and high-profit margins—continuing to fuel the traffickers?" Meghan asked.

"You can't. Which puts no end to this battle anytime soon." Ian turned to Meghan. "What about you? How are you doing?"

She shrugged a shoulder and took another sip of tea. "What you said is right. Seeing the rhinos affected by men's greed is difficult. But seeing a man shot over a rhino horn… It's hard to comprehend how something like that could happen."

"It is hard to understand," Alex said.

Meghan drank the rest of her tea, then washed the mug in the dish in the sink, fatigue clear in her eyes. "I'll see you both tomorrow. I'm going to check in on Kate to make sure she's okay, then crash."

"If you'll give me a minute, I'll walk with you as soon as I finish this last piece of milk tart." Alex still wasn't particularly hungry, but the tart was calling his name.

He tried to keep his voice even as he spoke so it didn't sound as though he was worried, but from the look on her face, he hadn't succeeded.

"Tonight scared me, Alex, but nothing's going to happen to me on the way to my chalet. Whoever was behind tonight's shooting is long gone."

"Maybe, but those three armed men were willing

to not only butcher the rhino but to shoot anyone who got in their way."

"Security is tight," she argued, "and I'm not the one they're after."

"Maybe not, but that doesn't mean—"

"I'll be fine, Alex." She zipped up the front of her jacket. "I'll see you both in the morning."

He watched her walk out the kitchen door. Tonight had stretched both of their nerves, but she was still his responsibility.

"I really don't think you have anything to worry about, Alex," Ian said once Meghan had disappeared from view. "Meghan's careful and, as she said, security's tighter than it's ever been."

"I know. It's just that..." Alex took a bite of the tart but could hardly taste it. It was his job to keep her safe, but somewhere over the past few days her safety had become personal to him. Too personal.

"When are you going to tell her why you're really here?" Ian asked.

Alex dropped the fork onto his plate. He'd asked himself the same question a dozen times over the past week. He didn't want to put her life in jeopardy by not making her fully aware of the danger she was in any more than he wanted to be responsible for sabotaging her relationship with her father.

"I'm trying to find a balance of following her father's request and doing my job to keep her safe."

"How many more days until the election is over?"

"One week."

"I've doubled the number of guards, which means staying here is probably about as safe as you can get."

"You're probably right." He glanced toward the door.

"Why don't you just go after her? You'll worry all

night, until you're certain she's made it to her chalet safely."

It was irrational to worry—he knew that Ian was right about the lodge being the safest place for Meghan, especially in the hours after an attack when the poachers would be keeping their distance to avoid detection. But irrational or not, he couldn't stop himself from worrying.

He'd been determined not to let this job affect him emotionally. Determined to keep his heart buried and safe. Meghan might be smart, pretty, funny…but none of those were reasons to get his heart involved. He'd done that once before and lost.

She'd died in his arms.

He had no intention of losing someone else on his watch. Or losing his heart again. All he needed to do was ensure her safety for the next seven days, then finish his contract while she finished up the project. Then he'd go visit his grandparents' farm and forget about the girl with the dark brown eyes and straw-colored hair that was trying to weave her way into his life without even knowing it.

"So you don't think I'm being paranoid?"

"Normally, I'd say yes. But tonight, one of my men was shot. One of my prize rhinos was almost killed, and the men behind it got away. Paranoid doesn't seem to factor into the equation right now. We're all going to have to be careful."

Meghan tried to shake off the terror that had moved down her spine and settled in her belly. Her hands were still trembling. Her breathing was still shallow. Poachers had already struck twice and now it had happened again. Except this time, she'd somehow stepped into the line of fire just by being in that Jeep. But even that reality seemed to pale beside knowing Oscar might not make it through the night.

And Alex's constant worrying didn't help. Somehow, he was convinced she wasn't safe, which only ended up adding to her fear. She shouldn't have walked out on him, but the combination of fatigue and out-of-control emotions meant she didn't have the energy to deal with his concerns. So she'd managed to convince herself—and him—that she was fine. Tried to convince him that what had happened tonight hadn't completely terrified her. That she could walk back to her chalet and no boogeyman was going to jump out of the bush and take her off into the night.

The only problem was, she was jumping at her own shadow.

If she believed she had no reason to be afraid, why was her heart racing and her palms sweating as if she'd just run a marathon?

Do not fear, for I am with you.

She hurried down the path toward her chalet, thankful Kate was finally feeling better, repeating the verse from Isaiah. Giving in to fear wasn't the answer. She knew that. But she wasn't sure she knew how to let go and trust.

I don't know how to do this, God.

No matter what had happened over the past couple weeks, what transpired tonight couldn't be ignored. The poachers might not be after her, but it showed how easy it could be to simply be in the wrong place at the wrong time.

"Meghan, wait!"

She stopped outside her chalet at the sound of Alex's

voice. Part of her had expected him to come after her...
had even wanted him to come after.

She turned around to face him. The night sky hov-
ered above them. This afternoon's rain had passed, leaving a canopy of brilliant stars above her. She could hear
the roar of a lion, sounding as if he was right here when
in reality the pride was probably a couple miles away.

She caught the concern in his eyes from the soft glow
of the lamppost and felt a stab of guilt for the way she'd
behaved earlier.

"I'm sorry." She shook her head. "I shouldn't have
walked out like that. Tonight... I don't think I've ever
been so scared. Oscar was the one who got shot, but
either of us could have been in his shoes."

"I know."

"All he was doing was defending that rhino's life.
Since when has someone's access to a drug become
more valuable than the life of another person?"

But it was. Ever since Cain had killed Abel over a
sacrifice, the lack of justice and evil had been all around
them. You could read about man's sinful choices and
their far-reaching consequences in every newspaper
and online broadcast.

She stood in front of him, shaking somewhat from
the cold but more from the fear that had taken hold.
She'd seen death in the wild. It was a necessary part
of life. But what had happened tonight was different.

"I didn't mean to scare you by worrying too much,"
he started.

"I know, but maybe you were right."

She hesitated at her confession. The lights along the
path revealed the man standing in front of her. His cowboy gear, blue jeans, belt buckle and a black T-shirt had

her mind scrambling to come up for air. But she also caught the concern in his eyes.

She swallowed hard. "I've spent most of my life having to be independent. I don't like feeling vulnerable and out of control. Trust...doesn't come easy. But tonight, that's exactly how I felt. Completely vulnerable."

"Maybe it's time you depended on someone. Trusted someone."

She'd never met a man who stirred her the way he did. "Who are you?"

"Your assistant," he teased. "Your gofer."

She couldn't help but smile. "That's not what I mean and you know it."

"I have three sisters. I might have been the younger brother, but I got used to watching after them growing up. Any boy who tried to take advantage of them learned to stay out of reach of my shotgun."

Her smile faded. "So you see me as a sister?"

"Yes—no. That wasn't my point. My point was simply that I feel an...obligation to make sure you're safe."

An obligation. So that was how he saw her. As a weak sister who needed the protection of a stronger, tougher brother. How very paternal of him. She frowned. She didn't exactly see him as a brother. Instead, he made her think of things like him kissing her—something very, very unbrotherly.

"Meghan—"

"I need to go to bed." She cut him off before he said anything else. Clearly she was the only one thinking those unfamilial thoughts. "I'll look at things differently tomorrow once I get some sleep. Nothing is making sense right now."

"Can I at least make sure everything inside your chalet's okay?"

She paused outside the door to her chalet. She'd placate him. Not because she thought there was anything to worry about, but because she was too tired to fight. She'd never worried about staying here. She kept her cameras and video equipment locked up in the main lodge. There was nothing of value here. Nothing to worry about.

She unlocked the front door, flipped on the light, then felt her heart plummet. Her normally neat room looked as if a troop of baboons had held a party there. Clothes were strewn around the room, couch cushions thrown on the floor, bedding tangled beside them. Nothing was in its place.

"Alex…"

"What's wrong?"

He looked over her shoulder, then pulled her behind him. "Stay here."

She didn't argue. All her thoughts of independence vanished. She watched from the doorway while he swept the one-room chalet and attached bathroom like a TV agent on some cop show, minus the gun. The kitchen window was open. She hadn't left it open. Or had she? She must have forgotten and walked out in a hurry without shutting it.

"There isn't anyone here."

"Look." She pointed to the open window. "I must have left it open."

It was the only explanation that made sense. The fruit bowl lying on the small counter had been knocked over, leaving oranges and bananas scattered across the tile floor. "One of the baboons must have snuck in here. They're notorious for making messes." She wanted so badly to believe that that was the explanation. But as her stomach dipped and her heart rate sped up, she couldn't shake off the sense that something darker had happened here. Something dangerous—and it wasn't over yet.

Alex shook his head, unconvinced at her weak argument. Meghan was meticulous. He'd seen it firsthand in her work. Everything she did, she checked and double-checked. She wouldn't have left the window open. Maybe this wasn't tied to the poachers, but there was no way he was going to buy that this was simply another coincidence.

"I think you're wrong. You're the one who warned me about leaving windows open. Tourists might forget that rule. Not you."

She pulled the window shut and locked it. "You have a better explanation?"

Maybe he could start by finding out if she could tell if anything had been taken. "A robbery? Do you notice anything missing?"

"I don't keep anything of value in here, so unless someone wants a couple pairs of flip-flops and an old safari hat, they're out of luck."

"What about your father?"

"My father?" Meghan picked up an orange and set it in the basket.

He was now treading on very shaky ground and he knew it. "You told me your father was an ambassador. Politics can get messy, especially with the corruption that runs deep in many of these countries. Maybe there's a connection there. When's the last time you spoke to him?"

"His birthday was three weeks ago. We talked via Skype for about thirty minutes."

"Did he share with you any problems with his job? Security issues at his embassy?"

"No. He's never been one to discuss his work. We talked mainly about my documentary. He seemed concerned when I told him about the recent rhino attack, but I assured him that, while it was horrible, the poachers were after rhinos. Not me."

So her father hadn't told her about the threats, hadn't even hinted that there might be a problem. That would make the conversation he'd soon need to have with her harder.

Tonight—baboons or not—changed everything in his mind. Meghan's life had to come above her relationship with her father. He was going to call her father, tell him what had happened and insist Meghan couldn't be left in the dark anymore. And then he was going to tell her the truth. But in the meantime… "We're going to need to call the police."

"What will they do? Dust for fingerprints?"

"Why not? It would be a start."

She dropped the rest of the scattered fruit into the bowl she'd been holding, then placed it back onto the small counter that held nothing more than a hot plate and sink. "We're talking about some stolen bananas? After dealing with a man who was almost murdered, I don't think they're going to care."

"Anything else missing?"

"I was serious about the bananas. I bought a bunch of bananas two days ago. Half of them are gone."

He rolled his eyes at her attempts at humor.

"Anything else?"

"It's hard to tell without going through things, but I don't think so." She shrugged. "I haven't heard of any other burglaries lately. I'll report the incident to Ian. Thieves hit the lodges from time to time, but I'll let him decide if he thinks it's worth getting the police involved. He'll probably agree, though, that it was just animals."

"Because a bunch of baboons is better than the alternative?"

She wasn't going to believe the alternative unless he told her the truth. But so far there was no hard evidence that anyone had followed through on the threats made against her. Every incident could be explained away by lack of maintenance, clumsiness or, tonight, baboons.

But if her father hadn't taken the threats seriously, he wouldn't have hired Alex to guarantee her safety. Which meant Alex couldn't assume anything. He was here because her life had been threatened, and it was time she knew the truth. It was time to call her father and put an end to all of the secrets.

TEN

Meghan set the basket of fruit into the passenger seat of the Jeep, trying to squelch the jumbled ball of nerves sitting in the pit of her stomach. The police had ended up returning to the lodge to talk with her about her trashed room, even though she'd assured them she'd accidently left open her kitchen window and was convinced a baboon had snuck in.

But the coincidences continued to pile up and even she wasn't 100 percent convinced anymore what was behind the incidents. All because of Alex. She'd never met a man who could be both completely charming and downright irritating at the same time.

Charming because he managed to make her heart pound every time she was around him. Irritating because he was so paranoid about the idea that she might be in danger…and because he managed to make her heart pound every time she was around him.

She let out a sharp woof of air. She couldn't remember the last time she'd let a man get under her skin. The past few years she'd dated a few guys, primarily from church, when she wasn't traveling. Nothing serious. No commitments.

But no matter how many times she'd told herself she

had no plans of falling for Mr. Cowboy, he'd look at her with those dreamy eyes of his and say something in that thick Texas drawl and before she knew it he'd reeled her in once again. Maybe Kate—and her constant teasing that Meghan had a Texas-size crush on Mr. Cowboy—was right after all. Because no matter how hard she tried to pull away, she was afraid she was falling for him hook, line and sinker.

Which was one of the reasons she needed to leave the reserve by herself for a couple hours this morning. She needed time to clear her mind and shake off the conflicting feelings that had her emotions spiraling out of control over the past few days.

"Hey."

Meghan looked up and frowned. Lost in thought, she hadn't heard Alex approach the Jeep. The last person she wanted to see at the moment stopped in front of her, wearing his typical cowboy garb complete with Stetson and huge belt buckle that looked so out of place in the African bush and its typical tourist garb and yet so…so Alex.

Her heart skipped a beat.

Meghan turned back to the fruit basket and started aimlessly rearranging the oranges.

"Going somewhere?" he asked.

"Yes, I need to run some errands in town." She glanced up at him. "Did you get my message?"

"That Oscar made it through the night and is out of critical condition, and we're going out to film right after lunch?"

"Yeah." Meghan dropped an orange into the food basket and looked up at him.

"Is everything okay?"

"Kate's better but asked me to pick up some medicine. I told Ian I'd visit Oscar, and on top of that, I just got a call from a friend of mine who's sick, so I'm taking him some food."

Meghan sucked in a deep breath. She was rambling like a schoolgirl. Nervous and edgy. Kate would laugh if she could hear her, tell her she was lovesick or enamored or some other ridiculous word—none of which was true. Meghan glanced up from the fruit basket and caught his gaze. Maybe if she kept telling herself it wasn't true, she'd eventually believe it.

"Meghan." Alex dug his hands into his jacket pocket. "After what happened last night, and with the police advising us to be extra careful, I don't think you should go out this morning by yourself."

"They didn't say we couldn't go out, just to be vigilant." She laughed as she dug the keys to the Jeep from her pocket. "You sound like my father. Worrying again. I'll be fine."

Her father had always worried about her safety. Throughout the years, he'd been known to hire private security details or cancel trips when he felt a threat from his high-profile job was serious. Nothing had ever happened.

"Until we know what hap—"

"I know what happened," she interrupted him. "Last night I left a window open and a baboon trashed my chalet."

"But we *don't* know that. Not for sure."

"Listen, I understand your concern, but I'm a big girl. For the past eight months, I've worked alongside a pride of lions in the middle of the bush. I know how to take care of myself. Besides, the poachers aren't after me."

"No, but I can't help but think of all the other things that have happened over the past couple weeks that *have* seemed to be targeting you. The collapsing of the hide, the accident with the Jeep, not to mention your room being trashed now. Even if all those things were nothing but flukes of bad luck, the poachers are real. They shot and almost killed someone, and there is no way to tell when they will be back."

She studied his expression. "Listen, I'll admit that last night scared me. A lot. But what am I supposed to do? I can't worry about every little mishap, and as for the poachers, I highly doubt that they'll be back. Security's tighter than it's ever been."

"Oscar's in the hospital because of those poachers. Is it really worth the risk of going out on your own until we know what is behind this?"

"Forget it, Alex." She climbed up into the Jeep and started the motor. "You're being paranoid. I'm going."

His hand still gripped the metal side bar of the Jeep. "Then at least let me go with you."

Seriously? The man never gave up. The main reason she was going was because she wanted time away from him to clear her head and figure things out. She might enjoy his company—a bit too much—and even secretly liked the fact that he worried about her, but she didn't need him looking over her shoulder every time she took a step.

She shook her head and revved the engine. "All I'm going to do is deliver a food basket, pick up Kate's medicine and check on Oscar. I'll be back in a couple hours."

"If you don't want me to come, then take Samuel. I'm asking you not to go alone. Just until we know for sure what's going on."

Meghan started to say something, then stopped. He was serious. "Samuel isn't paid to be my bodyguard. Besides, he left twenty minutes ago with a group of tourists and won't be back for a couple hours." She shook her head. Alex's job description included keeping video-footage records, taking photos when they needed him to and helping them keep up with their social media. It wasn't supposed to include worrying overtime for her. "Why are you so concerned? Every since you got here, you've acted more like my bodyguard than my assistant."

Alex's jaw tensed. "I'll make you a deal."

"What kind of deal?"

"Let me go with you, and I'll take you out to breakfast."

She laughed. "That's your deal?"

While her heart might long to say yes, breakfast with Mr. Cowboy wasn't exactly the prize she was looking for at this moment.

"Humor me."

She folded her arms across her chest and frowned. The man was incorrigible. She was going to regret saying yes, but arguing clearly wasn't going to work, either.

"You can come, and I'll take you up on the offer for breakfast, but only if you promise to quit worrying."

"Fine. I promise."

She waited for him to climb into the passenger side of the Jeep, hating the fact that a part of her was glad he'd managed to talk her into letting him come. So much for finding time to clear her head. If anything, it was more muddled than before.

He clicked on his seat belt and caught her gaze. "So is he a close friend?"

"Who?"

"The person you're taking the fruit to."

She tried to read his expression. Jealousy? More worry? She couldn't tell.

"I guess you could say we're close friends," she said. "His name's is Nathi and he's twelve years old."

Was that a sigh of relief? She couldn't help but smile. "Twelve?"

She pressed on the accelerator and headed for the front gate. "He comes around to the lodge a couple times a week selling vegetables. His parents died, so he lives with his aunt. Three months ago he was diagnosed as being HIV positive."

"Wow. I'm sorry."

"You don't think about the fact that he's sick when you're around him. He always manages to make me laugh. He's a good kid."

"Ian told me about the reserve's involvement with an effort to improve some of the local schools."

Meghan felt herself begin to relax. "There is a wonderful group made up from the community who help ensure students have the uniforms and supplies they need. I love the filming aspects of my job, but working with them makes me feel as if I'm doing something that really counts."

"Sounds as if you are."

Slowing down, she let a flock of speckled guinea fowl run across the road in front of them, wishing she didn't feel so glad he was with her. She stared out across the open veld, wind blowing through her hair, the crisp morning air filling her lungs, and let the soothing rhythms of the African bush help wash away the uneasiness that had settled over her the past few days.

Ten minutes later, Alex stepped out of the Jeep into the small courtyard of Nathi's compound. A rooster chased a hen across the recently swept yard, past patches of brown grass, rows of colorful plastic buckets and a broken-down car.

Alex followed Meghan into the sitting room of the whitewashed cinder-block house. Being with her underscored the decision he'd made late last night. As soon as he could get ahold of her father, he was going to tell the ambassador what had happened yesterday and insist Meghan be told why he was here.

For the moment, he shifted his focus to the room they'd just entered. The inside walls held traces of previous layers of paint: bright yellow, faded blue and an off-white. An old couch—cracked and worn—sat in the corner with a calendar and several drawings hanging above it.

Meghan sat down beside Nathi on the couch and gathered the boy into her arms for a big hug. He might be twelve, but he didn't look a day over eight. "Nathi, I've missed you."

"I've been sick," he began with his thick South African accent.

He tugged at the bottom of his faded SpongeBob T-shirt, showing off a toothy smile that hadn't faded despite the hint of pain in his eyes. Meghan settled in beside him, seemingly just at ease in a shanty as she was in the back of a four-wheel-drive Jeep filming a documentary that would be seen by thousands.

"Your auntie called me and told me you weren't feeling well," Meghan said. "Are you any better today?"

"Yes, but I did not go to school."

"I brought you some fruit." She nodded at the basket of fruit she'd set on the rickety coffee table in front of them. "Have you been taking your medicine?"

He nodded.

"Nathi, I'd like you to meet a friend of mine. His name is Alex Markham."

Nathi held out his hand as Alex sat down across from him on a wooden chair. "I am pleased to meet you."

"I'm happy to meet you, as well. Meghan told me on our way here that you're quite an artist."

The boy's smile broadened.

Alex pointed at the wall behind him to the drawings taped above the couch, black-and-white sketches of a dog, a colorful sunset and a chubby little boy.

"Is that your brother?"

"His name is Isaac. He's four years old."

"Miss Jordan was right. You're good."

"Mr. Markham's mother was an artist," Meghan added, "so he knows good art when he sees it."

Nathi's eyes lit up. "What did she like to draw?"

"Portraits and landscapes mainly. She was born in South Africa. Up in the north of the country. She died when I was twelve."

"My mother died, too."

"I understand how you feel." Alex leaned forward, surprised at the bond he felt with the young boy. "What's your favorite subject in school? Besides art."

"Science."

"Not girls?" Alex countered with a smile.

Nathi laughed and ducked his head.

They chatted over the next thirty minutes, about school, the puppy he was getting and the recent storm that had washed away part of the road near the river. Alex watched Meghan, enjoying the chance to see yet another side of her. The compassion in her voice, the interest in her eyes. And Nathi. The tragedies he'd already experienced in his short life had yet to put a damper on his outlook on life.

"Can we pray for you before we go?" she asked.

Nathi nodded as if it were something they were used to doing together.

Alex bowed his head, listening as Meghan prayed. Simple. Powerful. He believed there was a God, had committed his life to Him, but things had changed over the past year. He'd changed. He'd seen too much of the evil enveloping the world and at times wondered why God didn't step in to stop it. He'd watched families lose everything they had because of man's wickedness. Like when he'd lost Shannon.

He looked up at Nathi as Meghan finished her prayer, moved by the simple faith of a twelve-year-old boy suffering from the same disease that had taken his mother.

It reminded him that following God wasn't about going to church and checking off a bunch of boxes. It was about making a difference in the world because of your love for Jesus.

Which was exactly what Meghan was doing.

Alex raised his head at the final amen. Nathi smiled as Meghan gave him another hug and stood up.

Nathi turned to Alex. "Will you come back?"

"Of course." Alex nodded. "I'd like that."

"You will come on Saturday?"

"What happens on Saturday?" Alex asked.

Nathi's eyes widened as if he couldn't believe Alex hadn't heard about it. "It's a party. We will play games and eat sweets."

"Wow, that sounds like a lot of fun."

"Will you come?" the boy asked again.

"I don't know." Alex turned to Meghan. "You'll have to ask my boss."

"She is a tough lady, isn't she?"

"Nathi!"

The young boy smiled up at Meghan. "I am teasing. You are very nice."

"We're both coming." She looked to Alex. "But everyone has to help. For example, last year I did face painting."

"That sounds like fun."

"What can you do?" Nathi asked.

What could he do?

Alex's mind went blank. The only kids he was ever around were his nieces and nephews back in Texas that he saw three or four times a year. His sister Julia's girls loved tea parties and dress up, while the boys preferred video games and hunting. Beyond that, his experience with children was severely limited.

"I can make balloon animals." Alex spoke before he had time to process the question.

"Balloon animals!" Nathi clapped his hands together.

Alex frowned, worried about what he'd just gotten himself into. The last time he'd made balloon animals was when he was a sophomore in college. He'd thought it would be an easy way to impress a girl at a party for her little brother. The balloons had ended up being a huge hit. And so had Gregory Parker. Alex had spent hours practicing and still ended up losing the girl.

He cleared his throat. "The only problem is that it's been a few years, so I'm probably pretty rusty. My sister's girls always want to drag me into their playroom for a tea party."

"Now, that is something I'd like to see." Meghan laughed, clearly enjoying herself. "But the balloons will be perfect."

"Seriously, it's been a long time."

"Please?"

Alex caught Nathi's pleading expression. There was no way he could back out now. "I guess I'm in."

"Perfect." Meghan grabbed her bag off the couch. "We'll buy balloons in town today, and you'll still have three days to practice."

Three days? Right. And he'd been afraid he'd jumped in over his head when he'd agreed to be Meghan's bodyguard and gofer.

"And you, young man." Meghan turned to Nathi. "If you're going to be better by Saturday, you're going to have to eat lots of oranges, take your vitamins and rest."

Nathi smiled. "Yes, ma'am."

Five minutes later they were headed down the windy dirt road leading to town.

"He's a sweet boy," Alex said.

"Yes, he is. He never stops smiling. Never gives up."

"And the disease?"

"It seems to be under control for now. Relapses every now and then, but he's actually doing amazingly well for all he's been through."

Meghan pulled up in front of the restaurant and shut off the engine, hesitatingly briefly before getting out. "I'm finding it hard to imagine leaving here in the next few weeks. It's become more than just the documentary. I love my work, but the children have impacted my life in ways I never expected."

"It doesn't have to be the last time you visit."

"I don't plan for it to be."

He caught her expression before they headed toward the restaurant. She'd relaxed since agreeing to let him come with her, but he was worried about what her reaction would be when he told her the truth about who he was. Because his heart had just taken another giant step toward the edge of the cliff.

ELEVEN

Alex placed their orders with the perky waitress—
bacon, eggs and toast for him and a cheese omelet for
Meghan—then nodded as Meghan excused herself to
go to the restroom. He leaned back and took a sip of
his coffee. Besides them, a family with two small children and three older gentlemen drinking coffee, the
quaint restaurant was surprisingly quiet. The dozen
or so tables on the outside balcony overlooked a well-
manicured garden with a large fishpond, bordered by
tall palms and leafy shade trees.

He glanced at his phone sitting on the edge of the
table. He needed to hear from the ambassador, but
there had been no missed calls or texts. He'd left voice
mails and sent text messages, but so far had received
no reply. Which had him worried. He redialed ambassador's private line. If the phones were down in Equatorial Guinea's capital, there was the possibility that
the violence had escalated. He needed to know what
was going on.

He was about to hang up when someone finally answered. "Ambassador Jordan?"

"Alex. Good morning."

"How are you, sir? I've left messages and tried to
call several times but haven't been able to get through."

"I've been trying to call you, as well. Is everything all right with Meghan?"

"Yes. She's fine, but someone broke into her chalet last night. She's convinced she left a window and baboons got in, but—"

"You don't agree." Megan's father's words came out more as a statement than a question.

"No. It's possible, I suppose, but with the recent threats, I don't think we should take anything for granted. What I am sure of is that I need to tell her who I am and why I'm really here."

He grabbed his coffee and took a sip, waiting for the older man's response. As far as he was concerned, they were out of other options. Meghan had to know the truth.

"I agree," Ambassador Jordan finally said.

Alex let out his breath. "You do?"

"You sound surprised."

"Surprised and relieved. You've been so adamant this whole time that she not know, but with her safety clearly at risk, I don't believe we have a choice."

"Maybe I've been playing the fool trying to keep her in the dark. Trying to shelter her enough that she'd be able to believe that the threats really couldn't reach her. But you are right in that it wasn't baboons that trashed her room. Are you in a place where you can access the internet?"

"Yes. I'm having breakfast with Meghan at a local restaurant. She's gone to the restroom, but she left her computer with me."

"Good. I need you to check your email. I've just sent you a link to a YouTube video."

"Okay." Alex logged in to his Gmail account and

clicked on the link the ambassador had sent. "What is the situation there?"

"We've had some problems with the phones lines, which is probably why you weren't able to get through. There have been some demonstrations on the streets but thankfully, it's stayed fairly calm."

Alex waited for the video to load, then felt his jaw tense as he watched the first few seconds play. If there had been any question as to who had trashed Meghan's place, the evidence here meant there was no longer any doubt.

Someone stood inside Meghan's room holding a video camera while someone else trashed the chalet.

The messages her father had received were no longer idle threats. They knew how to get to her, and they'd just proved it.

"Where did you get this?"

"It was sent to me about an hour ago anonymously."

Cowards.

But cowards or not, they'd made their point. They were here. In South Africa. At the lodge. And they could get to her. The only other questions he had left to answer were which—if any—of Meghan's recent slew of accidents hadn't been accidents. And how far were they willing to take their threats?

"She needs to leave," her father said.

"I agree, but even with this, I'm not sure she will. This documentary is important to her, and she's almost finished."

"I need you to convince her to leave. This isn't worth her life. But if she does refuse, hire a couple more guards so she's protected 24/7. Money isn't an object at this point."

Meghan wasn't going to be happy about this, but her father was right.

Ambassador Jordon let out a deep sigh. "Let me know what she says and what you decide. And tell her... tell her that I love her."

A minute later Alex hung up the call. He had just pushed Replay when Meghan slid into her seat across from him, an excited smile on her face. He paused the video.

"Do you know what a genet is?" she asked.

"A what?" He tried to shift his focus from the video to her question.

"A genet. It's like a type of cat, but found in the wild. Covered with black spots and white patches, and it has a long, ringed black-and-white tail."

Alex glanced down at the frozen frame of her room being damaged and struggled to follow her train of thought. "No, I don't think I've ever seen one."

"They have one here. I just saw her. She's so tame, she steals people's food, and—" Meghan paused mid-sentence. "You're not listening to a word I'm saying. You okay? You look...upset."

"I'm sorry." He looked up and caught her gaze. "We need to talk."

She leaned forward, her eyes wide. "What's wrong?"

Alex tried to assemble his thoughts. Chasing down killers and bad guys was one thing. He had no problem with that part of his job. But the emotional side wasn't his strong point. He was going to have to give her the facts, state his case for her leaving, then listen to her response. Which wasn't going to be easy.

Please give me the words to say, Lord Jesus.

"I just got off the phone with your father," he began.

"My father?" Her eyes narrowed. "How do you know my father?"

"I'll explain everything, but first...first I need you to watch this."

He turned his computer so they could both see the screen and waited for the video to buffer again. She was still looking at him funny.

She stared at the screen, clearly puzzled, until the reality of what she was looking at dawned on her. "That's my chalet."

The footage of her room being trashed made Meghan sick to her stomach. Someone had been in her chalet. There were no excuses that could be made or assumptions that this was just another coincidence.

"I don't understand." She pushed Replay to watch it again, but even seeing it for the second time didn't alleviate the horror she felt. "I was sure I'd left a window open. That a baboon snuck in. But this..."

This terrified her. Two people ripping apart her chalet, one holding the camera, the other digging through her desk, her closet, pulling sheets and blankets off the bed.

"It wasn't baboons, Meghan. Two people took this video. They were there. The video doesn't really show enough to be able to identify them, but there's a chance they're staying at the lodge. Or maybe they just showed up on the property. Either way, they were there last night."

Which meant she had to question all the other things that had happened over the past couple weeks. Had they actually been more than just coincidences? She shook her head. None of this made any sense. "Why would someone do this? And my father...how's he involved?"

The waitress placed the hot food on the table in front of them, all smiles, and asked them if they wanted anything else. Alex thanked her and told her they were fine for now.

Except she wasn't fine. At all.

She stared at the yellow omelet with flakes of red and green peppers and felt her stomach turn. The photo of the omelet on the menu had made her mouth water. Now she didn't care. Any appetite she'd had walking into the restaurant had vanished.

"They sent the video," Alex continued, once the waitress had left, "to prove to your father that they could get to you."

"He sent this link to you?"

"Yes."

"How do you know my father?" Her mouth felt dry, like cotton. She reached for her glass of orange juice, accidently knocking it over with her shaky hand. She caught the glass as the sticky drink ran across the table, barely missing the laptop.

"I'm sorry."

"You're fine." He reached out to squeeze her hand. "This can be cleaned up. And we'll deal with the other issue, as well."

She set the glass back on the table. The waitress swooped in and began clearing up the mess. But just like the shooting last night, the implications of the video couldn't be easily mopped up. Her room had been destroyed. The video had been sent to her father as proof. And Alex knew her father.

She rubbed her temples with her fingers, then shook her head. A thousand questions swam through her mind. Why hadn't Alex told her he knew her father? Why hadn't her father told her there had been threats against her life? What would have happened if she'd been in that room when they'd come?

She looked up at him, unsure if she should be angry or afraid. "I need you to start from the beginning. Tell me what is going on. Why would someone do this, and how do you know my father?"

"I'll start with your father." Alex closed the lid on the computer. "We've never met in person, but we've spoken on the phone a number of times. I came here as a favor to him."

A favor? Meghan blinked, trying to absorb what he was saying. Her father had called in a favor to get Mr. Cowboy to...to what? To protect her? Be her personal bodyguard? Without telling her?

"Why?"

"He was concerned that your life was in danger."

Her mind flashed back to the fallen hide, the blown-out brakes on the Jeep, the trashing of her room. "And you are..."

"I'm a Texas Ranger—"

"A Texas Ranger?"

Meghan sat back, wanting to laugh. Sure that everything that was happening was nothing more than a very bad dream and she was going to wake up any minute. She'd joked about Mr. Cowboy watching too many cop shows—was she supposed to believe that he actually was one?

But as much as she wanted to laugh it off, his confession did answer some of her questions. Why Mr. Cowboy always seemed overprotective. And why he'd wanted the job with her team when he knew so little about making a documentary.

She swallowed hard, trying to ignore the sick feeling in the pit of her stomach. "Why did he hire you?"

"To keep you safe."

"From what?"

"Your father received threats related to the upcoming election in Equatorial Guinea. Threats that specifically mentioned you."

"It's not the first time he's received threats." Meghan pressed her hands against her pounding temples. "Why would he hide it from me this time? Why would you lie—"

"I never lied to you. I just didn't tell you the entire truth. I took this job to keep you safe."

"You left out a huge chunk of the truth. The fact that you're a Texas Ranger, for one. The fact that you're here working for my father. The fact that there had been threats on my life. Don't you think I deserved to know those things?"

"Your father asked me not to tell you. He thought he was protecting you...and your relationship."

Meghan blew out sharp breath of air. "Because it always comes back to what is best for him, doesn't it? Instead of just talking to me, he made the decision without even consulting me. Just like he always does."

She knew she sounded selfish and she hated it. She'd never stopped loving her father, but there were things Alex didn't know about their relationship.

"He just wanted you safe."

"He wanted to deal with the problem without having to interact with me at all."

Meghan shook her head. She knew her father. It had never been about her and her safety. Even as she thought that, the guilt surged. Maybe she wasn't being completely fair. Her father worked hard to represent his country, but work came far before family. Opening up to her about his thoughts and feelings—or even talking to her more than a handful of times a year—never seemed to make it onto his agenda.

Nothing had changed. Not when she was fourteen and her mother left, causing every emotion in her father to simply shut down. Not now.

Her gaze shifted to Alex with his apologetic expression, suddenly feeling embarrassed. He'd come to Africa for one reason and one reason only. Any ridiculous romantic thoughts that had surfaced on her part had clearly been nothing more than a figment of her imagination.

"The story of your mother," she began. "Is that true?"

"Yes. Everything I told you is true. She was raised in South Africa. I grew up on the family ranch back in Texas. I haven't changed anything about who I am."

Except for the reasons—those had changed, now that she knew the truth. All his attention and worrying over her was suddenly explained away into nothing more than a job. His questions, the reason he'd been out at night that time they'd laughed in the rain...his habit of always ensuring she was okay. She'd even noticed him making friends with the guards. It had nothing to do with him wanting to look after her because he cared for her. He'd just been doing his job. She shoved her plate toward the middle of the table. She'd have to deal with those feelings later.

"This video proves that they can get to me," she said. "Which means they're here."

"That's why I'm telling you. There is only so much I can do when you're unaware of what's at risk. I told your father you had to know."

"I still don't understand. Why hire you? What's your connection with my father?"

"Our fathers are friends. Forty years ago they went

up against rebel troops in Guatemala. Your father took a bullet for my father."

"So my father convinced yours to have you become my bodyguard."

"Yeah."

"Why did you agree?"

"My father's health isn't good—when he told me it would ease his mind if I'd do this favor for his friend, I was inclined to say yes. Besides, I've always wanted to visit my mother's homeland again. It's something that's been gnawing at the back of my mind."

She wanted to be mad at him, but he looked at her with those blue eyes that made her head spin. What right did she have to be angry? He'd just been doing his job. If she'd read something more into their interactions, then that was her fault, not his.

She stared out across the gardens and the lily pond, listening to the water tumbling over the rocks and trying to push away the implications. He wasn't falling for her. Just like she wasn't falling for him.

A bright red bee-eater with its black mask landed on the edge of the balcony for a moment. One of the children at another table ran toward it, scaring it away. It was vulnerable. She was vulnerable. This wasn't just about poachers or her being accident-prone. This was her life hanging on the line, making her feeling completely out of control.

Which was what really scared her.

When she was out in the Jeep watching the wildlife, she knew the risks. Stay within the safety parameters and chances were she'd be fine. A lion's behavior might not be predicable, but as long as she was careful, she felt relatively safe.

This situation was entirely different. Whoever these

men were, they'd been inside her room. Proved she was vulnerable. Proved they could get to her whenever and however they wanted and there was nothing she could do.

They were here. And she had no idea who they were.

But she had no plans to live in fear. She couldn't let them win.

"Why not just tell me what was going on from the beginning?" she asked.

"You'll have to talk with your father about that. He told me he was afraid you'd resent him if you knew why I was here."

"And that I'd send you on the next flight back to Texas?"

"I have a feeling you almost did."

She chuckled, because he was right. All her doubts as to whether or not he could actually make a documentary hadn't just been her imagination.

"I tried," she said, "but my boss didn't agree. My father clearly has connections."

"And he can be very convincing."

There were still so many things she wanted to know, but for now there was one thing she *needed* to know. "What exactly is at stake here? Clearly they were behind the attack on my chalet, but what else do you think they've done?"

"Honestly, I'm not sure. At first I bought into the idea that the threats were just hot air and that your string of accidents were just a coincidence. Some of what happened could have been due to lack of repairs around the lodge or, like the missing camera, somehow related to the poaching. But this video is proof that it wasn't a troop of baboons involved in trashing your room. And they sent the link straight to your father, so it must be connected to the threats he's been receiving."

The collapsing hide and even the Jeep she could explain away, but he was right. Someone had threatened her, that someone was here, and those threats were far from empty.

"Your father told me to tell you he loves you, Meghan. He wanted you to know that."

She looked away, the unwanted emotions of her and her father's relationship surfacing.

"Tell me about your father," Alex pressed.

She frowned at his persistence. "My father's career always came first. He lost my mother…"

She wasn't going to cry.

"And now he's afraid of losing you?" he asked.

"Maybe he already has. He's never been good at showing emotion, even before my mother left. We rarely talk. Rarely see each other." She struggled to put her feelings into words. "On some level I know he loves me, but…I don't know. He's never seemed to know how to show it. There was always something urgent, and I—I always felt like I was in the way."

"I don't know all the ins and outs of your relationship, but I know he loves you. He wouldn't have sent me here if he didn't."

"Maybe."

She wanted to believe him but wasn't sure she could.

"I think you should leave here, Meghan. Not permanently, just until the election is over, which means you could be back in a week or so."

She shook her head. "I can't leave."

"Why not? Put off the project temporarily and return with me to my father's ranch in Texas. Or we could stay in this country if you'd prefer. My mother has some relatives near Cape Town. You'd be safe there. No one would be able to connect you to them."

She understood his concerns, felt them herself, but eight months of footage and research were at stake. "If I leave now, everything I've invested over the past year will be lost. Any day now, Kibibi will begin the process of introducing the cubs to the pride. I know it sounds petty, and maybe even foolish, but it's important to me that I finish this project."

"Is it worth losing your life over?"

"Even with the break-in, these are still simply threats, Alex. Nothing more. No one has tried to harm me."

"What about the fallen hide and the brakes?"

"We can't know for sure they are connected. Surely if someone wanted to kill me, they could have already done that by now. What would be the point? With me dead, they wouldn't have any leverage. So they threaten. Make sure my father knows that they are there. Which simply means that, yes, I need to be careful, but I'm not ready to run."

"I can't protect you every moment."

"I know."

He sounded so worried that she had to remind herself that his protecting her wasn't personal. This was just a job to him. Which stung. Because no matter what her heart wanted to deny, Alex had become her anchor in the storm. She shook off the thought. She had to focus on the problem at hand.

"Because of the poaching, security at the reserve is high," she said. "It's got to be safer than most places."

"Even with all the extra security, they got into your room."

"I can move in with Kate temporarily so at least I'm not alone. Besides that—" she shot him her most persuasive smile "—I've got a bodyguard who's a Texas Ranger. Personally, I'd hate to be the one coming up against him in a dark alley."

"I don't know."

"Please, Alex. This is important to me."

He hesitated. "Fine, but as your bodyguard, I'm going to lay out a list of rules."

She nodded. "Whatever you say."

But she caught the doubt in his eyes and felt her resolve waver, hoping she'd made the right decision.

TWELVE

Meghan was still contemplating whether or not she'd made the right decision to stay as she parked in front of the hospital. Maybe Alex and her father were right. Maybe she should leave. Disappear until the elections were over. But running seemed like the coward's way out. And she wasn't ready to throw away almost a year's worth of work because of a handful of threats. Being brave wasn't really a part of the equation, but giving in would mean the bad guys had won and she'd lost.

Besides spelling out his list of rules, Alex had said little on the drive from the restaurant, making her wonder if he was regretting agreeing to let her to stay. But Oscar getting shot had nothing to do with her or her father. It had simply been a matter of him being in the wrong place at the wrong time. And while watching the video of her room being trashed had scared her, it didn't mean that her life was in danger. At least, that was what she wanted to believe.

Alex had made his position clear, though, with his list of rules. One, she wasn't to go anywhere alone. Two, every night she would stay with Kate with a hired night guard outside the chalet. Three, she wouldn't go out filming without Samuel or another *approved* armed guard with her at all times.

She knew he was doing his job and not just being paranoid, but she'd yet to wrap her mind around the fact that her "gofer" had just become her bodyguard. Or rather, that he'd been her bodyguard all along without her knowing. She glanced at his profile, wishing Mr. Cowboy—or should she say Mr. Texas Ranger?—didn't cause her heart to stay in such a constant state of flux.

Meghan grabbed the potted yellow orchid she'd picked up at the local florist's in town and headed into the hospital with Alex. Once inside, they found the room Oscar was sharing with three other patients, glad to see him awake. The latest report from the doctor was that while Oscar was finally out of the woods, a complete recovery was going to take several weeks.

She set the plant on the small table beside Oscar. "How are you feeling?"

"I am in some pain, but I know I'm lucky to be alive." Oscar looked at Alex. "They told me you saved my life."

Alex shook his head. "I'd call it teamwork. Samuel drove us here, Meghan arranged the medical care, and God looked out for us along the way."

Meghan nudged Alex with her elbow. "It also helped that Alex is actually a Texas Ranger from the Lone Star state. Something I just found out today."

Oscar smiled. "Like Chuck Norris?"

So even Oscar had heard of Chuck Norris's famed TV show from the nineties.

"Just like Chuck Norris," Meghan said.

Alex groaned at her response, but she wasn't going to let him off the hook that easily.

"Something like that," he said. "Though I'm not nearly as famous."

"You will be famous now." Oscar's grin broadened. "You saved my life. My family will be here soon. They will want to thank you."

"We're just glad you're going to make it," Alex said.

Tears pooled in the man's eyes. "Last night I believed I would never see my family again."

"We wanted to come see how you were doing, but there's also another reason we're here." Meghan pulled up a chair beside the bed and sat down. "I know you've already spoken to the police, but Alex would like to ask you some more questions about the shooting."

Oscar shifted gingerly in the bed, careful not to pull on the IV connected to his arm. "The police must find whoever did this, but I don't know anything."

"For now, just go over what happened again with us," Alex said. "How much do you remember of last night?"

"Only small things."

"Let's start slowly, then." Alex grabbed a second plastic chair and sat down beside Meghan. "Last night, after we pulled you into the Jeep, you kept saying that someone was after you. We want to figure out who was out there and who shot you."

Oscar's smile faded. "I had gone out on night patrol with three other guards. We split up into pairs so we could cover more territory. It is our job to check the perimeter, ensure the safety of the rhinos and watch for any signs of poachers."

"And last night?"

"We saw one of the fence lines had been cut. When I rang Ian, he told us that one of the rhinos hadn't moved in four hours so he wanted us to go check on it."

"Did you find the rhino?"

"Yes. Thankfully, it was sleeping and seemed fine."

"What happened next?"

"We were headed back out on patrol to check on a second rhino when we heard another vehicle. One of the security teams had been having trouble with their radios so we thought it could be them, but with all that is happening, we follow up on everything."

Meghan caught the grimace in his expression. "Are you hurting?"

"The medicine is wearing off."

"Do you want me to get the nurse?" Meghan asked.

He shook his head. "They'll be in soon with more."

"So did you go off on your own?" Alex asked.

Oscar nodded. "The brush was too thick to drive through at that point so I left my partner with the truck. I didn't plan to go far. Just far enough to see who was there. I was careful, as rangers have been shot, mistaken for poachers, in the past. We always identify ourselves and keep track of the security teams as well as who is out on the game drives for the evening."

"But it wasn't one of the security teams you found out there."

Oscar shook his head. "It was three men carrying rifles, but there wasn't enough moonlight for me to catch more than glimpses of their faces."

"And they saw you?" Meghan asked.

Oscar nodded. "And shot at me, but at first, they missed. I ran, but in the confusion, I ran the wrong direction, away from my partner."

"What did you do next?" Meghan asked.

"I stopped for a moment, knowing I had to figure out where I was. Knowing I needed to get to the lodge. Then I saw your vehicle. I knew the men chasing me were still behind me and that my only chance was to make it to your vehicle."

Which was when he'd been shot, once he'd left the protection of the bush for the open road.

"There is one other thing I've been thinking about since the police left." Oscar tugged on the bedsheet covering him. "I might be wrong, but…"

Alex leaned forward. "Sometimes it's the smallest detail that ends up turning a case around."

The ranger nodded. "I worked in Zambia for many years, where there was a problem with poaching elephants. It was a challenge for us then, but things are different today."

"In what way?" Alex asked.

"Poachers used to go in, shoot the elephant and steal the tusk with little risk of being caught. But today, the risk is much greater."

"Because of all the security in place?" Meghan asked.

"Yes. In our reserve alone, we have GPS trackers, armed rangers and security guards, with plans of implementing dog handlers, thermal-vision goggles and tracking chips. But in a number of killings, it's being reported that these security measures can be used to kill the rhinos instead of protecting them."

Meghan shook her head. "How?"

"Take the two rhinos who were killed on our property, for example. No matter what we do, the poachers always seem to be one step ahead."

"Which points to the possibility that someone on the inside is feeding the poachers information," Alex said.

"Exactly. To find a rhino without inside information would be almost impossible, but they can pay a ranger three or four thousand dollars to use a cell phone to alert a poacher to an unguarded rhino or simply look the other way. It makes their job a whole lot easier."

"Do you have a name? Anyone who you suspect could be passing on this information?"

Oscar's gaze dropped. "It's only a feeling. I don't want to get anyone in trouble."

"Who do you think it is, Oscar?"

"His name is Dominick. He's one of the rangers, but he is not always where he is supposed to be. I could be wrong, but he buys things none of us can afford."

"I'll make sure the police look into his background discreetly."

A nurse stepped into the room, wearing a stark-white uniform. "I'm sorry, but I'm going to have to ask the two of you to leave. It's time for some pain medicine so our patient can rest."

Alex stood up beside Meghan. "We will look into this, but if you think of anything else, please let me know."

Oscar nodded. "I will. And please. Find whoever did this."

Alex walked past the row of patients who were sitting along the wall of the narrow outer corridor of the hospital as they waited to see a doctor. He tried to process Oscar's theory. Meghan had first mentioned the possible connection of insiders involved in the poaching. In reading more online about the poaching issues, he'd found several articles that pointed to people within the industry—those supposedly involved in wildlife conservation—being implicated in the rhino-poaching rings.

"What Oscar says makes sense, Alex. The missing camera in a spot where no one would think to look unless they already knew it was there, the GPS tracker showing the poachers were near that rhino—someone could be feeding poachers information from the inside."

"I agree." He stopped to face her beside the row of cars outside the front of the hospital. "I'll contact the police and have them look into Dominick, but if there really is an insider involved, what about Ian? He's the most obvious, the one with the most to gain."

"No way." Meghan shook her head. "I've worked with him and his wife for the past eight months and I can't see him compromising what means so much to him and his family. He loves this land, the animals and the people here."

Alex continued toward the Jeep beside her, still not convinced. "Everything you've just said could be motivation in itself. With the economy down, you mentioned that the reserve is facing financial issues. Maybe Ian even fears he could lose the reserve if things don't turn around. Now take the poachers. They're well financed, but they need someone, like Ian, to ensure they stay in business. Right or wrong, it becomes a win-win situation for everyone involved."

"I still don't agree." Meghan climbed into the driver's seat and shoved the keys into the ignition, but she didn't start the engine. "If we're looking at an inside job, I think we're looking at one of the rangers—like Dominick—or a staff member."

She might be right, but he'd seen far too many men who worked on the principle that the ends justified the means. Most of them hadn't started out intending to sell their souls, but a man's integrity could be twisted and broken if he thought compromises would save him in the end. The problem was, in the end, they never did.

Alex clenched his hands in his lap, wondering if he should even bring up the other idea gnawing at the back of his mind. "There is one other issue to consider, but you're not going to like it, either."

"Wow." She shot him a wry grin. "You're really on a roll today, aren't you? But I have a feeling you're going to tell me what you're thinking whether I'm going to like it or not."

Alex smiled back. She was right. "I've been doing some research since I got here. Equatorial Guinea is one of a number of countries that has become a haven for traffickers—anything from drugs to humans to wildlife. While the current president has been working with the UN to help enforce stricter laws against all forms of trafficking, the new regime trying to take power in next week's election has known ties to an international crime syndicate."

Meghan's eyes widened. "Now you're really stretching things. You're telling me that the poaching that has been going on here is somehow related to the threats against my father and whoever trashed my room?"

"I think it's a possibility."

Her smile was back, taking his heart by surprise. "So what would Chuck Norris do, Officer Markham?"

"I'm serious," he countered.

Her smile faded. "I still think you're stretching the connection."

"Maybe, but I'm trained to look at all the possibilities, which is exactly what I'm doing."

Meghan slowed down and pulled off onto a narrow paved road. "We need to get back to the lodge so we can film this afternoon, but first I want to show you one of my favorite places."

A minute later she stopped the Jeep in front of a fenced-in, small wooden building.

"Where are we?" he asked.

"This is one of the two hides on the reserve that overlook the water."

He followed Meghan between two chain-link fences to the wooden structure that stood on stilts above the water. A board creaked beneath him as he stepped into the hide.

Alex hesitated. "Are you sure this is safe?"

"Ian assured me just yesterday that both hides had been checked and repaired."

"Wow." Alex ducked down to look through the wide opening in the front, then sat on the bench overlooking the slow-moving water. "I can see why you like it here. This is stunning."

He hadn't expected the assortment of wildlife. Trees, reflected along the water's edge, held huge birds' nests. Since his arrival, Meghan had shared a wealth of information, teaching him not only about the mammals they encountered but the vast diversity of birds. She'd taught him to identify herons, fish eagles, warblers and yellow-billed oxpeckers. They'd clearly barely scratched the surface.

Alex took the binoculars she'd handed him and honed in on a small bird with a bright orange beak and chest and a blue back sitting on a thornbush. "What is that one called?"

"It's a Malachite Kingfisher."

Two hippos grunted in the middle of the pool, only their ears and the tops of their heads visible above the surface. Beyond the hippos, a crocodile lay on the far bank, sunning itself.

"I could spend hours out here." She put the cap back onto her camera. "But for now we should get back. I need to check on Kate and then we need to track down Kibibi. I just thought you'd like to see this."

"I do. Your love for the bush is starting to rub off on me."

She laughed, but there was a new reserve to her countenance. He studied her face, trying to read her expression. Fatigue showed in her eyes, but it was more than that.

"About everything that happened today," he began. "I'm sorry. Sorry that I wasn't able to be up-front from the beginning with you. Sorry that you are having to go through this at all."

"It's not your fault. You were just doing what my father wanted."

"He loves you, you know. That's why he hired me."

She looked up at him and caught his gaze. This time it was doubt he saw in her eyes.

"He hired you," she said, "because he prefers delegating problems with me so that he doesn't have to interact with me himself."

"I don't understand."

Meghan stood up and headed back to the Jeep.

He went after her. "Meghan?"

"All he's ever done is pay someone else to fix my problems. There was boarding school when he wanted to be free to travel more, or a hired nanny during holidays because he was busy." She stopped at the Jeep and leaned against the hood. "This situation is no different. He arranges for a Texas Ranger, along with a couple of guards, to protect me, thinking it will make everything okay. He's never realized that the only thing I've ever wanted from him was for him to be my father."

THIRTEEN

Meghan thumped on Kate's door with her elbow while balancing a tray of food she'd picked up from the kitchen. A moment later, Kate opened the door, wearing a pair of Mickey Mouse long-sleeved pajamas, hair pulled back in a ponytail and her nose still red from blowing it too much.

"Thought you might like some homemade soup and fresh bread." Meghan set the tray down on the kitchen counter, then turned to her friend. "How are you feeling?"

"I know I don't look like it, but I'm actually feeling tons better." Kate took the lid off of the bowl and breathed in the aroma. "And this smells delicious, which is a good sign. I haven't been able to smell anything for days with this cold. Plus, I'm actually hungry."

"Getting your appetite back is a good sign. So does that mean you're up to going out with us this afternoon?"

Kate set her hands on her hips and cocked her head. "Are you really missing my company, or are you having trouble with Mr. Cowboy?"

"Very funny, Kate." There was no way she was going to admit that going out again alone with Alex had her almost as worried as running into the poachers. Somehow knowing who he really was had changed everything.

"I'm kidding, and you know it. I just don't think I'm strong enough to even walk to the Jeep at this point, but tomorrow for sure. I'm about to go stir-crazy locked up in this chalet." Kate grabbed a spoon and sat down in front of the tray. "Though to be honest, I'm not sure I want to be out there, either. After last night, I'm finding myself jumping at every little noise."

"Brace yourself, then." Meghan popped open the tab of the pineapple soda she'd brought for herself. "Because there's more to the saga."

Kate's face paled. "Another rhino was killed?"

Meghan briefly explained the threats, her vandalized room and the fact that Mr. Cowboy was really a Texas Ranger.

Kate's jaw dropped. "I'm not sure what surprises me the most, that someone trashed your room or that Alex is a Texas Ranger."

"I'm still trying to take that one in, as well. But what I really wanted to say is that I hope you're up for company for a few days. With all that has happened, Alex is insisting I stay with you, along with a hired guard outside the chalet at night."

"I actually think that's a good idea, and I've got room." Kate nodded at the extra twin bed against the wall. "But I'm wondering if you should go out at all. This sounds serious, Meghan. Though somehow I have a feeling that having your room trashed isn't the only thing you're afraid of."

Meghan frowned. Kate could be far too perceptive at times. Her feelings toward Alex had her wanting to run. But she wasn't sure she could put her feelings into words at this point. "It's nothing to worry about."

"Like I believe that."

Meghan grabbed one of the bread rolls from the tray. She did need someone to talk to, and Alex certainly didn't fit the bill.

"When I'm out there in the bush filming, or editing, or in discussions with video crews back in the States, I'm this confident person who knows what needs to get done. But when it comes to my heart…it's an entirely different matter."

Kate blew on her soup, then took another spoonful. "We all have our stories of broken hearts, Meghan. The key is finding out how to deal with those fears and not let them stop you from moving on."

"I could really use some advice."

Kate set her spoon back in the bowl. "I never told you about Kevin."

"Who's Kevin?"

"My ex-fiancé left me at the altar a year and a half ago."

"You never told me that you were engaged. That's horrible."

"Yes, it was. He ran off and married my best friend, who would have been my maid of honor at our wedding. I always thought the story would make the perfect script for a romantic comedy if it had a different ending. Something along the lines of 'jilted bride finds love with lonely best man' or something like that, but in my case, there was no lonely best man or happy ending. Just a lot of embarrassment and explanations as to why my fiancé was honeymooning with my best friend."

"Ouch."

Kate took another sip of her soup. "Now it's your turn. What has you running scared every time Mr. Cowboy looks at you with those luscious eyes of his?

Because, trust me, if I were you, the last thing I'd be thinking about is running."

"Luscious eyes?" Meghan groaned at the comment. "Please."

"You can't blame a girl for noticing. Now, be honest."

Meghan nibbled on the bread, unsure how *honest* she wanted to be on a day that already had her feeling exposed.

"Okay, I'll admit that his eyes are a bit…luscious." She paused, hoping that talking about it would help her to put things into perspective. "But part of me isn't convinced I'll ever find anyone who loves me enough to stay around for the long haul."

"Because of your parents."

Meghan nodded. "My mother chose another family over me. My father chose his career over me. I've always felt as if I was battling against the odds when it came to relationships."

Those losses had affected her relationships with men. Not all marriages ended the way her parents' marriage had. Not all mothers walked out of their daughters' lives, and not all fathers put their careers before their families. So what was wrong with her that she'd never been reason enough for anyone to stay, to try to make things work?

"So their decisions left you feeling as if you're not worthy of being loved?"

Meghan tried to swallow the lump in her throat. "I guess that pretty much sums it up. I was the little girl always waiting for someone to choose me—and most especially for my mother to come for me."

"But she didn't."

"No." Meghan took a drink of her pineapple soda, then set the glass down. "She and her new husband were killed in a drunk-driving accident on their way home from dinner just a few months after she left. So, no. She never came back."

"You never told me that part of the story."

It was the hardest part to remember. Faded memories of her mother drifted through her mind. They'd been few and far between. Some good, like nighttime kisses and bedtime stories. And others not so good. Like the loneliness of boarding school and knowing her mother would never be there to talk with her about clothes and boys. "It's easier just to say it was a long time ago and brush it off, but her leaving did affect me."

There had been very few people in her life she'd let glimpse into her heart. A handful of girlfriends throughout the years, her aunt Rita and lately Kate.

"Maybe we're all searching for love in our own way," Kate began. "I always thought I had the 'perfect' family, but I was the plain Jane and knew I wasn't perfect. Still, I kept trying to portray that image. I ended up battling with my self-esteem and trying to find someone who'd love me. I thought things were different with Kevin. Turns out, I was wrong."

"Have you ever got past his leaving you?"

"Some days it's hard. I have to consciously remind myself that my identity isn't determined by who I'm with, but by the One who created me. That, more than anything, is helping me put the past behind me."

"That's pretty profound."

"I also had to accept that Kevin is with the right woman. It's still a struggle sometimes to believe that there's someone out there for me, even though I wasn't the one for Kevin." Kate pushed her bowl back and looked at Meghan. "So what is it about Alex? What makes you push him away?"

Meghan wiped the bread crumbs off the table, then brushed them onto the tray. "A lot of things. From the start, he's made me feel vulnerable. But now I'm thrown by the fact that I think I read him completely wrong. All this time, I thought he was protective of me because he cared for me, but now I know that he's simply a cowboy who came to save the maiden in distress as part of a job. That means he doesn't feel the same thing I do."

"How does he make you feel?"

She didn't have to close her eyes to see him.

"Comfortable. Happy. He's the first person in a very long time who has made me want to stick around and take a chance."

"Maybe there's your answer."

"But—"

"No buts. No excuses, Meghan. You can't let your past dictate your future. I spent years chasing the wrong kind of love. You can spend your whole life running away from love, but I don't think either option is right."

Meghan wrapped her fingers around the soda can. "I hardly know him."

"So you guard your heart and let him walk away? Then you'll definitely lose him." Kate shook her head. "Because that's what happens when you guard you heart and don't take a chance."

Alex viewed Kibibi and her four cubs through the camera lens in the passenger side of the Jeep while Meghan videotaped the scene with two cameras. One was positioned on a tripod, strategically placed outside the Jeep, the other she held where she sat beside him. They'd spent the past two hours slowly following the family through the bush, but the anticipation that they might be joining the pride anytime soon ended when Kibibi stopped for a nap in the afternoon sunshine.

But despite Meghan's disappointment, the interaction between the lioness and cubs amazed him. The affection Kibibi displayed toward her cubs as they nuzzled against her, playing with her tail and with each other until three of the cubs fell asleep beneath the cloudless Africa sky, was unexpectedly moving.

Meghan switched off the camera and stretched her legs while the three cubs slept. The fourth still played, batting at his mother's tail as she flicked away the flies. The mood in the clearing—and in the Jeep—was peaceful and calm. He'd discovered early on that making a documentary was far less glamorous than he'd imagined, but the chance to get to know Meghan had made up for the hours of waiting for those perfect shots. This afternoon, though, she'd said little beyond giving him a few photography tips along the way.

He pulled out a ziplock bag of trail mix his sister Julia had sent with him and offered Meghan some.

She picked out three honey-roasted pecans and popped them into her mouth.

He stared at the bag, shaking his head. "You know, you're not supposed to do that."

"Not supposed to do what?"

"Pick out your favorites."

"You mix everything up?"

"Yeah. It's called trail *mix.*" He dug out a small handful from the homemade combination of dried pineapple, banana chips, pecans, M&M's, pumpkin seeds and almonds and ate them in one bite.

Meghan's nose wrinkled.

"You're extra quiet today."

She looked up at him, her canvas safari hat blocking

the sun that had already left a trail of freckles across her nose. "I guess I'm still trying to sort through everything that has happened the past couple days. Between Oscar being shot, finding out there have been threats against my life—not to mention the discovery that my assistant is actually here to be my bodyguard—yeah, it's all thrown me for a bit of a loop."

"Even I wasn't expecting a situation like last night."

For him, the shooting and the destroyed room had raised his assignment to a completely different level. No longer was he looking at a situation that could be explained away by a handful of coincidences. He'd gone from babysitting the ambassador's daughter to full-blown, around-the-clock security detail.

"It's normal to be scared, Meghan"

"Good, because I *am* scared, and worried, and mad. And I feel like I should be doing something—anything— to track down the people behind this instead of just sitting around waiting for them to attack."

"We are doing something."

"Like?"

"For starters, I've contacted a friend of mine who works with the State Department to look into the threats that have been made against you and your father. I want to know that a full investigation is being made at that level."

"You think it could be someone working for my father who's involved?"

"It's possible. I've also been in contact with an employment screening service that is performing background checks on all the employees here at the reserve to see if we can find a connection there, and I've spoken to the local police detective about the ranger Oscar told us about."

He'd also spent a lot of time praying that they'd find an answer soon.

She reached into the bag and grabbed a small handful of trail mix, then proceeded to eat it one ingredient at a time. "So is this how you normally spend your day as one of the famed Texas Rangers? Watching over vulnerable females—minus the pride of lions in the background, of course?"

Alex laughed. "I'm not sure that either *normal* or *famed* describes my life, and no, it doesn't always involve vulnerable—albeit beautiful—females like yourself."

"Oh…you saved yourself on that one." Her smile was back. "So what do you usually do?"

He stared out across the open spot where Kibibi and her cubs slept. "My primary role is criminal investigation. While I've worked a number of cases over the past year, most of my time was tied up on a tough case, tracking down a man who killed half a dozen people across Texas in a seven-week killing spree."

"I remember reading about that case when it made the headlines. The death toll was horrible."

"It was, especially for me. While I've always managed, for the most part, to keep work separate from my personal life, this case was different."

"What made it different?"

"The case became…personal." Alex hesitated, not sure he wanted to dredge up memories better left buried. "Not only were we trying to stop a ruthless, dangerous man from killing again, but I was in charge of keeping one of the witnesses safe."

She studied him, eyes narrowed slightly, lips pursed as if she were trying to read his thoughts. "Who was she?"

"Her name was Shannon."

He'd already said too much. He didn't want to talk about Shannon. Didn't want to remember about the last day he'd seen her. They'd called him to tell him there had been a murder, but he'd arrived too late to save her. He was there when the medical examiner drove away with her body. Had watched her parents bury their only child. He'd never been able to shake off the guilt of losing her.

"Did something happen to her?"

He picked up the camera and focused in on Kibibi with the zoom as she yawned, baring her teeth, before rubbing her face against one of the cubs who had just woken up. "Why would you think that?"

"Since the day you arrived, your concern over my safety has seemed...very personal. As if you feel you have to make amends for something."

He wasn't ready to admit she was right. "I always take my jobs seriously."

"Maybe, but it feels like there's more to it than that. As if there's something you want to prove by keeping me safe. Something that has made this job personal."

"Being here has felt personal."

Because of Shannon. Because Meghan was right— he *had* wanted to prove to himself that he could do this job, that he could keep someone safe.

And because of Shannon, he'd tried not to fall for Meghan. There was no way to deny that Shannon now made up a part of who he was. Knowing her had changed his life. Losing her had cost him part of his heart and made him cautious about loving again.

But a long time had passed, which was why, today, he was more aware of how the woman sitting next to him had changed him. How she'd managed to dig through those thick barriers around his heart he'd tried to set in place after Shannon's death.

"Did you love her?"

He tipped his head to block the dropping sun, avoiding her gaze. "I was in love with her. Shannon had witnessed one of those murders and was planning to testify."

"What happened to her?"

Alex closed his eyes for a moment. No one had blamed him for her death, but that didn't mean he'd forgiven himself. He'd promised to protect her. Had assured her that she was safe.

"She was being kept in a safe house until she could testify. Stamos found out where she was and killed her."

"I'm sorry."

"Later it was proved he'd paid someone off to find out where she was."

"Stamos was arrested, wasn't he?"

"It took over a year, but yes. He's on death row now, awaiting his execution. He'll never hurt anyone else. But his arrest was too late for Shannon."

The months after Shannon's murder had passed like a blur. He'd spent every waking moment tracking down Stamos. Putting him in jail had given him the justice he'd been after but not the satisfaction he'd hoped for, because even his arrest couldn't take away the lingering emptiness. Or the regret that he hadn't been able to save Shannon. Her death had been a major factor in his burnout and, for the first time in his life, had him thinking about an early retirement.

"Tell me about her."

"Why?"

"Because I sense that she was—at least at one time—

an important part of your life. Our past makes us who we are, both the good and the bad."

"She was smart, beautiful and sometimes too serious."

Like someone else he knew.

"Someone told me recently—i.e., Kate—" Meghan said "—that you can't let your past dictate your future. Sometimes you have to let that past go."

"Sounds awfully wise."

"Let's just say it's something I'm trying to figure out, as well."

He studied Meghan's face, her long hair pulled back in a loose ponytail and those bright brown eyes looking to him for answers. After years working as a Ranger, he'd learned the necessity of separating himself emotionally from his work, because he knew that getting personally involved only complicated things. Keeping everything at an arm's length allowed him to look at situations objectively and do his job the way he was trained.

But Meghan had waltzed into his life and made him realize that something was missing. Made him want to forget his determination to control his emotions and give his heart another chance with love. And he knew what he wanted to happen next. He wanted to pull her into his arms and kiss her. To tell her that he was falling for her...had already fallen for her.

Instead he lifted his camera and turned back to the cubs who were now waking up. That wasn't the answer she was looking for, and he didn't want her to end up like Shannon. He didn't want to lose her.

FOURTEEN

Alex finished twisting the long balloon into the shape of a sword, then gave it to the chubby boy of seven or eight who smiled up at him. He'd spent the afternoon making balloons and handing out food to the seventy-five children who were clearly enjoying every moment of today's festivities. Those festivities had included three-legged races, water-balloon fights and—the biggest hit of the day so far—a giant homemade piñata filled with candy.

The boy scurried off with his sword, only to be replaced by another boy asking for a sword. Alex blew up the balloon, then twisted it into the fairly simple shape he'd managed to master over the course of the day. Except for his sisters' kids, he'd never spent a lot of time with children, but clearly balloon animals crossed all boundaries of culture and language.

He finished making the handle, then gave it to the boy, reminded again of how much had changed since he first arrived. He'd come to Africa for two reasons. One, to fulfill his commitment regarding Meghan's safety. The second reason was to once again visit his mother's homeland. But something else had happened since he'd arrived.

For months, he'd struggled with his faith. He'd seen so much evil over the past decade—and especially the past year—that it had finally left him feeling empty and burned-out. He spent his days trying to keep crime off the streets, but he'd grown tired of the constant fight for justice. Tired of feeling that while they might be winning some of the battles, the bad guys were winning the war.

But, like a camera, Meghan had managed to zoom in on the important things for him to remember. In the midst of threats on her life and poachers, she'd reminded him that there was still good in the world. And as with Nathi, she'd reminded him that sometimes it was the smallest things that in turn made the biggest difference.

He'd watched her all afternoon, looking perfectly at home with the kids in a pair of jeans and a yellow-and-gray-striped T-shirt, her smile never leaving her face.

He grabbed the last pink balloon, blew it up and started shaping it into a crown, then headed over to where she stood by the drink table, passing out drinks and chatting with the kids, who clearly loved her.

Alex walked up to her and handed her the balloon. "For you, my lady. It's a princess crown."

She laughed and set the pink creation on her head.

"I see you've made a few new friends today." She pointed to a couple of the boys swinging their swords together until one of them popped, evoking a string of laughter as they ran off together.

Alex couldn't help but smile. "I admit when I first got roped into the project I was convinced I'd made a huge mistake, but I'm glad they are enjoying the balloons."

"And I'm glad you decided to join us."

"Me, too. And as for you, you look like you're enjoying yourself."

"I am." She filled another plastic cup with water and handed it to one of the girls. "Being around these kids reminds me of what is important in life. Politics and disasters will always take over the headlines, but sometimes it ends up being the simplest things in life that really matter."

Squeals pulled his attention to the soccer field. In his bright orange T-shirt and with a large smile on his face, Nathi was running with the ball.

"Go, Nathi!"

Alex watched as Nathi ran down the field with the ball, but his heart was focused on the woman standing beside him.

Meghan cheered on Nathi as he approached the goal. At the last second, he kicked it too far to the left, missing the chance to score. The ball rolled off into the field. Nathi scurried after it into a patch of tall yellow grass blowing in the afternoon breeze.

Meghan turned to get one of the girls a drink, then stopped at a high-pitched scream. Nathi had fallen on the uneven ground and now sat holding his leg. Dropping the empty cup, she ran across the field to where he sat and knelt down beside him.

"Did you sprain your ankle?"

Nathi looked up at her. His eyes were wide and filled with terror. He shook his head.

"Nathi? What's wrong?" Meghan studied his leg. Blood trickled down his calf beneath two fang marks.

Meghan felt her lungs constrict.

Alex was right behind her. "Meghan?"

"It's a snakebite." She turned back to Nathi. "I need you to try to relax. We'll get you to the hospital, and you'll be fine."

Alex started pulling off Nathi's shoe and sock.

"Meet me at the Jeep." Meghan jumped up. "I'll go grab the keys."

Alex scooped up Nathi and started carrying him while Meghan ran back to the table where she'd left her bag. Inside, she fished for the keys, trying not to panic.

Kate ran up beside her. "Do you want me to come?"

Meghan shook her head. "I think it's better if you stay here with the kids. They've looked forward to this day for a long time. Maybe you can serve the afternoon snacks as a distraction." Meghan finally found the keys. "And have someone call Nathi's aunt. She needs to know what has happened."

Kate nodded as Meghan run for the Jeep.

Alex was ready with instructions. "Sit with him and keep him as quiet and still as you can. I'll drive. Make sure you keep his leg lower than his heart."

Meghan nodded, trying to remember what Samuel had taught her about snakes. Her fear, though, wasn't just about the bite but also the possibility of secondary complications.

Alex flew down the road while she held on to Nathi.

"How serious is this?" she asked Alex.

"I don't know. His body is already weak. You need to start praying."

"I am." She ran her fingers across Nathi's face and brushed off a patch of dirt from where he'd fallen. He'd had so much fun today between playing soccer, crossing swords with his friends and even running in the three-legged race.

"Stay with me, Nathi.... You're going to be okay." He nodded at her, the fear still evident in his eyes. "The doctors have antivenom and antibiotics to treat you with."

Meghan grabbed her phone off the seat beside her and called the hospital to let them know they were coming, wanting to believe her words that he would be okay.

Please, God, this sweet little boy has already come so far. Please let us get there in time to save him.

Five minutes later, Meghan was shouting for someone to help as Alex ran beside her with Nathi in his arms to the front of the hospital. Dr. Archer exited the front of the hospital and hurried toward them.

"Bring him in. We're ready for him."

The doctor started shouting instructions to his staff.

Meghan kept up beside them as they transferred him to a gurney and hurried down the breezeway. "Please tell me he's going to be okay."

"I'll let you know as soon as we get him stabilized."

Meghan watched them wheel Nathi into the emergency room. The panic from when Oscar had been shot had returned. "I certainly didn't plan to be back here again so soon."

"Me, either."

Oscar had continued to improve and was supposed to be released later today. Now they just needed another bit of guidance from God to help a friend survive.

"You okay?" he asked.

"No, I'm frustrated." Meghan sat down on the bench beside him and leaned back against the wall, her nerves about to snap. "Nathi's already faced so many difficulties. It's hard to see him have to deal with something else."

"I know, but I have to say, today's made me think about something."

She looked up at him. "What is that?"

"Too often we blame God for all the problems we face. At least, I've found myself doing that. Last night

I read a few verses in James where it says that religion that God our Father accepts as pure and faultless is—"

"—to look after the orphans and widows in their distress and to keep oneself from being polluted from the earth." Meghan finished the verse for him.

"Yeah. I think I've tried to make my faith too complicated. I watched you and Kate with the kids today and realized how easy it is for me to focus on what's wrong out there to the point that I forget to see God's hand. Because no matter what is happening around us, He *is* still here. He knows that there are children who've lost their parents, and widows who feel left alone, but God is still God and He wants to use us to be His hands and feet in their lives."

She knew he was right. God didn't leave just because something went wrong. He was right here in the middle of this messed-up, crazy world, using people willing to make a difference for His glory.

"You're the one sounding wise today," she said. She sucked back the tears, needing to blow her nose and find a way to pull herself together. "I'm going to go to the restroom. I'll be back in a minute."

As Meghan walked, she wiped the back of her hand across her face, brushing away the tears. Nathi had wedged his way into her heart over the past few months; his smile and the quiver in his chin when he laughed were all so dear to her.

Still, Alex was right. Bad things happened, but God was still God.

She walked down an empty breezeway and realized she'd taken a wrong turn. This section was still under construction, with plans to open next month.

For a split second she wished she'd asked Alex to come with her. Which was silly. Only those at the school knew she was here—a handful of teachers, Kate and Ian. She was safe and needed to stop looking for trouble around every shadow.

A woman stood at the end of the breezeway. There was something familiar about her. It only took her a second to place her. She'd been staying at the lodge on her honeymoon. She and her husband came from somewhere in Eastern Europe.

"Excuse me?" the woman said. She started walking toward Meghan.

"Can I help you?" Meghan looked around, wishing it wasn't so quiet.

"You work at the lodge."

"Yes."

"My husband and I are honeymooning and he came down with some nasty stomach bug. I'm trying to find the pharmacy."

"This wing is still under construction. You'll have to go back to the main part of the hospital, which is down this breezeway and to the left. The pharmacy is there."

"Thanks."

Meghan smiled back at the woman, shaking off her ridiculous suspicions of being watched and followed. There was nothing to be afraid of.

"There is one more thing," the woman said as Meghan turned away. "I don't think you've met my husband."

"Your husband?" Meghan shook her head, not understanding the sudden change in the woman's expression.

She was grabbed from behind. A man wrapped one arm around her neck, the other around her waist. Held this close against him, she could smell the terribly familiar scent of cigarette smoke on his clothes.

"I wouldn't scream if I were you," the woman said

calmly. "My husband tends to have a bit of a nasty streak."

Meghan tried to pull away from him, but his grip on her was too tight. "What do you want?"

"We thought that the video would be enough motivation for your father but, apparently, we were wrong."

"I don't understand."

"Oh, I think you do, Miss Jordan. Your father apparently doesn't like to play by our rules—which is a pity."

The woman took a step forward and shoved something over her face. Meghan tried to identity the penetrating smell as she struggled to break free—nail-polish remover, starter fluid… Her mind wasn't working properly. She felt herself falling, then slipped into nothingness.

FIFTEEN

"Tell me, Meghan Jordan, how smart is your father?"

Meghan opened her eyes at the voice and squinted in the sunlight. She blinked, willing her eyes to focus on the man standing over her. She remembered him from the lodge—bald, unshaven, and wearing khaki pants and a button-up shirt. Head pounding, she blinked again, trying to understand why her hands felt anchored behind her.

"Well, Meghan?"

She shook her head. "I don't know. I don't understand the question."

She tried to remember what had happened. Maybe their car had been in an accident, and her father... He'd said something about her father. Was he here? No. He couldn't be.

She blinked. Where was Alex?

"Where's Alex? We were at the hospital together."

"Alex isn't here, sweetheart."

His tone mocked her. A sliver of fear snaked through her. She tried to get up, then realized her hands were tied behind her. Whoever this man really was, he wasn't here to help her. She shifted her focus to her surroundings, trying not to panic. They were outside. She was sitting on the ground, leaning against something. She turned her head and caught sight of the rim and tires of a blue car. Behind the man was a sugarcane field. The only sounds were the pounding of her heart and a half-dozen birds chirping in the top of a tree.

"You tied me up."

"Didn't want you to run off." He leaned closer until she could smell his tobacco-soured breath. "I'll ask you again, then. How smart is your father?"

The fog holding her brain hostage was slowly starting to lift. She caught the man's frown and tried to put together the pieces of a jumbled puzzle. She'd been at the party for the kids. Nathi had been running, chasing the ball...

He'd been bitten by a snake.

Alex had rushed them to the hospital. The doctor had told her to wait outside. She'd headed for the bathroom. The hall had been empty. Or at least she thought it had been empty. Someone had come after her. A man... and a woman.

She looked up, squinting into the sun and saw the woman standing to her right for the first time. Tall, thin, familiar. The honeymooners from the lodge. They'd grabbed her—pressed something against her face.

"Can't answer my question, Meghan?"

She fought to focus. "My father's smart. He's an ambassador."

"Which makes you the ambassador's daughter and, in this situation, a valuable commodity. So here's how it's going to play out."

A commodity?

"I still don't understand. I have no connection to my father's work. I don't have any information, so I don't see how I have any value except—"

"Except in his love for you. And a father's love for his child can come in very handy sometimes."

She forced her mind to work. "So the brakes on the Jeep, the hide that collapsed—and my chalet. All were attempts to show how easily you could hurt me to keep him in line and so he'd do what you wanted."

He looked at the woman. "She is smart. Almost as clever as her father after all. Except all of our little reminders weren't enough. Your father still isn't playing fair."

"What do you want him to do?"

"You don't need to worry about that."

If this was about her father, then it was connected to the threats. She needed to understand what they wanted, but more importantly, she needed to escape. Moving only brought with it a sharp pain radiating through her stomach. She squeezed her eyes shut against the pain.

"My advice would be to not try to get up."

Her jaw tensed. "What do you want now?"

"It's simple." He held up his smartphone and snapped a photo of her. "Now for the video segment. Tell your father he needs to follow our orders if he wants to see you again. We're done playing nice."

She stared at the phone.

"Tell him."

Meghan fought back tears. "Daddy, they took me. I don't know what they want now, but please—"

The man pressed a piece of duct tape across her mouth before she could finish her sentence. Together, the two of them lifted her into the back of the car and slammed the trunk shut.

Alex rushed down the outdoor corridor of another wing of the hospital. Unlike where they'd dropped off

Nathi, this wing was vacant of people and eerily quiet this late in the afternoon.

Where was Meghan?

An uneasy feeling nudged him forward. Something wasn't right. It had been almost fifteen minutes since Meghan had gone off in search of a restroom. It wouldn't have taken him that long to start looking for her if the doctor hadn't come by to talk to him about Nathi's prognosis. It hadn't been until the doctor had finished telling him they expected a full recovery barring any reaction to the medication they were putting him on that Alex had glanced at his watch and realized Meghan should have been back by now.

Realized he never should have let her go off alone.

He quickened his steps until he was running down the corridor. The woman's restroom loomed ahead at the edge of the newly constructed wing. "Meghan?"

He pounded on the entrance, still calling her name. No answer. He shoved open the stall doors one by one. If she'd been here, she was gone. Which made no sense. She wouldn't leave without him. Wouldn't leave without knowing how Nathi was. Wouldn't have left on her own.

Which meant someone had taken her.

Alex pushed back the thought. He was being paranoid. Maybe there was another way through the hospital corridors. She'd probably gotten distracted. Perhaps she'd run into someone she knew and had stopped for a chat, or decided to take some photos.

But his gut told him his paranoia wasn't off base this time. Meghan was in trouble.

He ran through the waiting area to the small parking lot. The Jeep they'd come in was still parked beneath the shade of a row of trees. People came and went. A guard sat in a wooden booth reading a newspaper.

Out of breath, Alex approached the guard. "I'm looking for an American woman. Hair pulled back in a ponytail. Fair skin. She was wearing—" what had she been wearing? "—a pair of jeans and a yellow-and-gray-striped T-shirt."

The man dropped his paper into his lap. "I think I saw her."

"Where did she go?"

The man pointed toward one of the exits that led out of the parking lot. "She left a few minutes ago with a couple. They were helping her out. Practically carrying her. She looked pretty sick."

Helping her? It sounded more as if she'd been drugged and abducted by the couple. Anger seeped through him. No one would have done anything to stop them, because they would have assumed the couple was helping her.

"Can you describe the couple? Their car?"

"They were white…both had dark hair. The drove off in a four-door car, I think. Green—or maybe blue?"

Alex clenched his fists at his sides. He was no longer being paranoid. He'd let his guard down and now Meghan's life was in danger.

Who had her, and where would they take her?

He pulled out his cell phone and punched in Ian's number while walking the perimeter of where the guard said she'd been. Ian would still be at the school, helping to finish up the festivities with the students. That meant he was less than ten minutes away. And he had contacts with the local law enforcement.

Something pink caught his eye while he waited for Ian to pick up. He bent down toward the thorny bush. Meghan's pink zebra cell phone. She must have dropped it while they were carrying her out.

He picked it up, then turned the phone over in his

hand. He'd smiled when she'd told him her favorite color was pink. Meghan wasn't embarrassed that she loved to read romance novels or watch chick flicks, or that she could maneuver the African bush like an expert. She'd love his sisters, and he had no doubt they would love her.

But first he had to find her.

Ian finally picked up.

"Ian. It's Alex. Nathi's going to be okay, but Meghan's missing. I think…I think someone took her."

Kids shrieked in the background. "What?"

Alex heard the tension in his own voice. "She's been kidnapped, Ian."

He explained what had happened as quickly and concisely as he could, including the guard's account and finding her cell phone. The bottom line was that the threats her father had received were being realized.

"Stay at the hospital. I can be there in a few minutes, and I'll call a friend from the police department, let him know what has happened. I'll ask him to meet us."

A moment later, Alex hung up the call, hating the feeling of helplessness that engulfed him. Standing around doing nothing wasn't his M.O. He held her phone between his fingers. He couldn't call her. Had no way to track where she was. But he had to do something.

He looked around him. A handful of people walked past him. Patients, family members bringing food, hospital staff… Someone had to have seen something.

Ten minutes later he was still waiting for Ian and didn't know any more than he had when he'd called him.

He let out a deep sigh. He'd never been big on words, but now he wished he'd told Meghan what he felt about her. Because for the first time since Shannon died, someone had managed to take his heart captive. Her disappearance made him realize how important she'd become to him. There was no way to deny the truth anymore. Meghan wasn't just another case he'd been hired to work on.

Which seemed crazy.

But from the first day he'd met her, there was something about Meghan that was different. She'd made him laugh again. Made him believe that maybe—just maybe—there was someone out there worth taking a risk on.

He paced the circular driveway in front of the hospital, feeling helpless to do anything. He should never have let her talk him into allowing her to stay at the reserve. If they'd gone to Cape Town or Texas...

But there was no way to know if that would have been enough to keep her safe. Meghan had been certain that no one had any reason to seriously hurt her. He could only hope she was right. All he did know was that he was the one who was supposed to protect her and he'd failed.

Just like he failed with Shannon. His stomach tensed. *God, this can't happen again. I can't lose her.*

He wished he had the resources he did back home. He glanced at the main entrance of the hospital. No cameras. No team of security guards. Which left him with few if any leads.

Because, for all practical purposes, Meghan had vanished.

Meghan's head smacked against the top of the car trunk as she tried to sit up. She wanted to scream, but her mouth was covered in tape. Regardless, as far as she knew, they were in the middle of nowhere. Even if she could scream, no one would hear her except her captors. After shoving her into the darkness of the trunk, she'd heard them speaking in whispers until their voices had faded. It had sounded as if they were speaking German, or maybe Dutch? She wasn't sure.

Then they'd left her alone. Terrified.

She shifted her legs, trying to find a comfortable position. She should have listened to Alex and her father. Taken the threats against her more seriously. She could have left until the elections were over, but now... now it was too late.

Whatever was going on, the threats, kidnapping and possible ransom were far beyond anything she knew how to deal with. She had to get out of here before whoever had taken her returned. She pulled on the binding on her wrists until the skin felt raw. Tears welled in her eyes. She wasn't going anywhere.

Meghan licked her dry, cracked lips, and panic seeped through her veins. She might have traveled the world and grown up independent, but that didn't make her brave. Not when it came to this situation. Funny how the only thing she'd ever really worried about on her travels was catching some exotic disease. She'd never imagined being the pawn in a political game.

Regrets surfaced one by one. Regrets toward her father over the lack of forgiveness and understanding on her part. Why did it take facing the end of her life to put things into perspective? Why was it that she had to come face-to-face with losing someone before she realized how much he really meant?

She wanted—needed—the chance for them to start over. She needed to call her father. Ask him to forgive her. Maybe she hadn't been the only one in the wrong, but at this moment, that didn't seem to matter.

She continued working to loosen the rope, her mind wandering back a dozen years. When she'd become old enough to understand what her father did for a living, she'd worried about him being killed in the line of duty. Eventually, she'd been able to accept that he'd chosen a life of risks to serve his county. He performed that service quietly and competently, without much fuss or fanfare but with strong integrity and dedication.

Now that she thought of it, his parenting style was quite similar. Long speeches and emotional overtures were not his forte, but he'd always been someone she could rely on utterly and completely. Had she taken that for granted?

Maybe his reasoning for bringing in Alex had not been to push her away, but to keep her safe. What if she'd missed his intentions all along? This time, anyway, while she'd tried to downplay her father's fears, they'd clearly been right.

And then there was Mr. Cowboy. Alex had swept into her life like a rugged Texas Ranger hero out of a romance novel. He'd managed to take her heart and turn it inside out. From the moment she'd jumped into that Jeep to avoid a charging rhino, she'd realized there was something different about him. Something worth exploring despite her heart's trepidation.

But she'd continued to push him away, when all her heart had wanted was to give him a chance. He had become the white knight who always tried to rescue her, but she'd let fear take over.

And now, if he didn't find her, she might lose him forever.

I'm not ready to die, Lord. Not yet.

She closed her eyes and tried to concentrate. She needed to figure out where she was. To get out of this trunk. A plane sounded overhead. The airport? Was that where they had brought her?

A knot of fear wound its way through her. If they left the country, what were the chances that anyone would find her?

Not this way, God. Please. Help Alex find me.

Voices whispered in the distance, growing louder. They were back.

Before she could explore her feelings any further, she needed to find a way to get out of there alive.

Ian arrived at the hospital with Kate and a Detective Anders from the local police department.

"Ian briefed me on the way here as to what's happened," the detective began. "Kate had a recent photo of Meghan on her cell phone. We've sent it out to all of our officers. We're canvassing the area and setting up police checkpoints on the roads out of town."

"What about the airport?" Alex asked.

"There's an airstrip five minutes from town," Ian said. "I have a friend who works there. I'll call to see if there are any planes scheduled to take off." He pulled his phone out to make the call right away.

Alex knew the risks. The first moments after a kidnapping were crucial. Already, close to thirty minutes had passed.

"A man and a woman are scheduled to leave for Johannesburg in a private plane within the next fifteen minutes," the detective said to them a minute later. "Here is something else. The description I was just given matches the description from the guard at the hospital."

Alex felt his blood pressure rise. "If they take off with her on that plane, tracking her down is going to be difficult."

Flight plans could change. If Meghan got on that

plane, they could lose her. But he refused to accept that would happen this time. He had no intention of losing the woman he was falling in love with.

Meghan's head felt detached from her body. They were moving her, but she couldn't tell where. She was still battling the effects of the drug they'd given her and the fog it had placed her in. She'd heard another airplane take off, which had to mean they were close to the airport. She'd been there once before and knew that the airport was nothing more than a single hangar beside a strip of tarmac. Nothing more, really, than a landing strip in the middle of an open field. But it meant they could take her anywhere, which would make her almost impossible to track down.

They'd send the photo and video message to her father, demanding he follow their instructions or he'd never see his daughter again. Her father cared. She knew he did, but would he choose her over what he felt he needed to do for his work?

It was the question that had always haunted her. She'd always worried that she'd stood in the way of his duty. That her presence had always held him back from moving forward. That secretly he'd wished her mother had taken her so he could focus on his duties to his country.

What if she'd been wrong?

Alex had spoken of forgiveness. Assured her that her father had loved her.

Now she'd do anything to have him standing with her telling her that. Now all she could do was pray she'd get the chance to tell the two men in her life what she felt. Forgiveness and acceptance for her father. A chance for love with Alex.

SIXTEEN

Alex pressed his foot on the accelerator of the Jeep, neck and neck with the small plane headed down the runway for takeoff. Only one thing mattered. Meghan was in there, so they had to stop the plane. He shifted gears and pressed harder on the gas. Tarmac was running out. He eased forward. The plane swerved to the right and bumped off the tarmac, coming to an abrupt stop in the middle of the field. Three police vehicles pulled in beside him, making certain the plane would be unable to divert around him to take off.

Alex jumped out of the Jeep as six armed officers surrounded the plane with orders that the passengers inside exit the plane. A moment later the ladder on the plan lowered and a couple exited the plane.

"They were guests at the lodge," Alex said.

"Convenient." The detective held up a photo. "Interpol has them listed as Tobias and Sari Radu from Romania. Apparently weapon and human trafficking wasn't enough, so they wanted to try their luck with wildlife."

"I'd say it didn't turn out too lucky for them."

The truth was about to come out, but right now all Alex wanted to do was find Meghan.

He ran up the steps and into the small cabin. "Meghan?"

Silence greeted him. Where was she?

He hurried down the narrow aisle of the plane, then shoved open the bathroom door and stared into the mirror, his heart pounding with fear. The plane was empty. *No!* Alex hurried out of the plane back onto the tarmac. He had to find her.

He grabbed the shirt of the handcuffed man and shoved him into the stairs. "Where is she? Where is Meghan?"

"I do not know." The balding man tried to pull away, but Alex kept his grip. "There must be some mistake. We don't know anything about this…woman you seek."

"Let him go, Alex."

Alex hesitated at the detective's order, then pulled back, hands up, restraining the urge to punch the man. "You took her. You were seen leaving the hospital with her. There were witnesses."

"There has been a mistake. We are simply here on holiday. I'm sure all of this will be cleared up soon."

"He's lying."

Alex's cell phone rang and he dug it out of his pocket and started walking down the tarmac to take the call. A minute later, Alex hung up and stepped back in front of Ian and the detective.

"That was a man I hired to look into the background of you and your family," Alex began. "He had some interesting news for me."

"Our backgrounds?" Ian asked.

"I had to know who was behind this."

"And you thought I was involved with poaching my rhinos? No. Never."

"I know that now—but your brother-in-law is."

"Wait, no. Not Hendrik." Fear registered in Ian's eyes. "This reserve is a family business. He would never sell us out."

"It's a family business that's struggling financially." Alex's jaw tensed. It never ceased to amaze him how far people would go for the sake of financial gain. "But we don't have time to argue. We need to find Meghan."

"Where is he right now?" the detective asked.

"Back in Joburg," Ian said. "If he was here, he would have told me."

Alex shook his head. "He's here. My contact just talked to your sister-in-law. You've got roadblocks set up, Detective?"

"Yes."

"Good. They're sending me the information on the car he rented. We need to find him, because I'm pretty certain he's working with these two and that he has Meghan."

They found her in the trunk of Hendrik's rental car at one of the police roadblocks fifteen miles away. By the time Alex saw her, she was sitting in the back of one of the police cars looking dazed. Alex slipped into the seat beside her. She was cold, her body shaking. "Are you okay?"

She nodded. "They gave me some…some drug to make me sleepy, but I am okay…now that you're here."

He started rubbing her arms, trying to get her to warm up, then took off his jacket and pulled it around her shoulders.

"It's over, Meghan. You're safe now. They've arrested everyone involved. Apparently Hendrik had gotten involved with a major supplier of illegal horns. The Romanians were here to get a piece of the action. Your father became involved because of his stance against animal trafficking in a country they were using as their transit base to smuggle the goods between countries."

He shot up a prayer of thanks. Thankful she was okay. Thankful there hadn't been a bloody standoff. Thankful at the moment for so many things.

She looked up at him, eyes wide. "I was so scared."

"I know, and I'm so sorry you had to go through this. I never should have let you out of my sight."

"This wasn't your fault. There was no way to know who was behind it." She let out a sigh and then seemed to brace herself. "Is Ian involved?"

"As far as I can tell, no." He brushed away the tear sliding down her face. "Did they hurt you?"

She shook her head. "They grabbed me from the hospital and put me in the trunk. If you hadn't got here in time, they would have killed me."

"That didn't happen. Oh, Meghan, I was so afraid I'd lost you."

"Like Shannon?"

"No. Not like Shannon. She's a part of my past—she always will be—but you're my future and the only one I see right now."

She wrapped her arms around his neck, smiling for the first time since he'd found her. "You never lost me. I knew you were out there looking for me. I knew you would find me."

He pulled her closer, tilted her chin, then pressed his lips against hers, needing to convince himself she was real and here with him. That he hadn't lost her.

"Alex? Is she okay?"

Kate stood in the doorway of the vehicle, interrupting the moment. But there would be more moments like this. He was going to make sure of that.

"She will be."

"The ambulance is here. They want to take her to the hospital to check her out."

Alex slipped from the car with Meghan as Ian stopped in front of his handcuffed brother-in-law.

"How could you do this?"

Hendrik shook his head. "You just don't get it, do you?"

"Get what?" The pain from his brother-in-law's betrayal was clear on Ian's face. "The fact that you were undermining everything I've worked for over the past two decades? Everything your father and your grandfather built up on this land? The fact that you not only slaughtered precious animals, but killed anyone who got in your way? And what about Annabet? When she finds out what you've done... Explain to me why you would do something like this."

"You always were too sentimental, Ian. You look at this land as a legacy. I look at it as a business. Every year the money we bring in is barely enough to cover the bills. Something had to be done, especially when you decided to go and start a conservation program, hire someone to produce a documentary and fund school programs to help the community. All very noble plans, but they're also extremely costly. Something you clearly don't think about. I found a way to save everything."

"And what about Meghan?" Alex spoke up for the first time. He didn't even try to stop the anger filtering through his words. "Explain how she fit into all of this."

"We need to keep the right people in power in certain places in order to keep doing what we do. And if we have to do a bit of manipulating to tip the scales... well, I'm not above using some political influence to get what I need."

"Let me ask one more thing, before they haul you away. How big is this?"

Hendrik smiled. "Big enough that you'll never be able to stop it."

Two days later, Meghan crouched in the thick grass beside Alex and held her breath. Kibibi cautiously approached the pride with her four cubs. It had been almost thirty-six hours since Hendrik and his team had been arrested. Six more people had been arrested for their involvement in several hundred incidents of poaching. Meghan had slept most of that time, trying to shake off the effects of the drug they'd given her. When she'd finally gotten up, she'd received a call from Samuel. He'd tracked Kibibi heading for the pride.

Her fingers gripped the edges of the camera as she captured the scene while Kate handled a second video camera set up at a different angle, ten yards to their right. The first meeting with the pride—and the cubs' father, Jama—could go either way. Kibibi walked in front of the cubs, trying to sense Jama's reaction. In an encounter between a cub and a four-hundred-pound male, a moment of aggression could maim or even kill.

Jama lifted his bulk off the ground and stood, towering over the cubs. He batted at the smallest one, knocking him into the dusty ground, while the rest of the lions watched. Kibibi started toward Jama as one of the cubs pulled at his mane, but Jama leaned over and nuzzled the cub.

For the moment, the danger seemed to be over. Which only added to Meghan's own sense of relief. Relief that Nathi and Oscar were going to be okay. Relief that her life was no longer in danger.

"Hard to believe this is over and I don't have to look

over my shoulder anymore." Meghan continued photographing as she spoke.

"Hendrik was right about one thing," Alex said. "Someone else will take his place—the operation is too big to end with just a few arrests."

"But it's still a step forward in stopping them."

All three of her captors would be facing charges of kidnapping, in addition to trafficking and animal-rights violations. Only one of the charges was being disputed. Hendrik blamed Meghan's kidnapping on his partners, saying he'd had no idea she'd been in the vehicle. For now, it would be up to the courts to decide.

"What happens now that you have the final piece of your documentary?" he asked.

"I'll spend the next few weeks editing with Kate and wrapping up here."

"And your father? Have you talked to him yet?"

"I spoke with him on the phone this morning. As soon as I'm done here, he's planning to meet me in Cape Town so we can spend some time together."

"How do you feel about that?"

"The last couple days have made me realize that I need to forgive him and try to make our relationship work."

"What do you think he'll do next?"

"He's actually thinking about retiring and moving back to California. He has a sister there and they've always been pretty close." She turned to him, trying to read his expression. The taste of his kiss still lingered on her lips. Leaving South Africa behind wasn't the only thing that was going to leave a hole in her heart. "What about you? I guess you'll be going back to Texas in a few days."

"This job was only temporary. But before I leave…

we haven't had time to talk about what happened between us."

"When you kissed me?"

She'd worried that he'd been motivated only by the intensity of the moment. That he didn't really share the feelings spiraling through her. But that kiss on the plane had erased any doubts about how she felt. He might have started out being nothing more than a temporary protector and bodyguard, but he'd become far more than that in her mind.

"Meghan, I'm not good at verbalizing how I feel, but when I agreed to take this job, I came here hoping to find the piece I thought was missing in my life. I believed it was my mother's heritage in this country. But I was wrong."

"What do you mean?" Meghan asked.

"I know this sounds crazy, but that missing piece in my life…is you."

Meghan had all but forgotten about Jama and the cubs now sleeping in the morning sunshine. "No. You don't sound crazy at all. I've spent my life running, but you make me want to stop and take a chance."

"You make me laugh, Meghan. You made me realize what is important in life again. I'd become so burned-out and disillusioned, but now I'm engaged in life again—I just can't picture it without you. You make me stronger, make me want to strive to be the man God wants me to be, because I've completely fallen in love with you, Meghan Jordan."

She stared into his blue eyes, and all the fear she'd bottled up evaporated into the morning sunshine. "It's going to be complicated. I'll be traveling the next few months, and I'm not sure where my next job will take me."

"Shh…" Alex pressed his finger gently against her

lips. "We can use Skype and email and text until you finish up here and figure out everything else later."

The next thing Meghan knew he was kissing her beneath the warm African sun, making her forget about all the promises she'd made to guard her heart. Making her believe she'd found someone she could spend the rest of her life with.

She breathed in his essence. Part cowboy. Part hero. A man she could trust and who made her feel worthy of being loved.

SEVENTEEN

Three months later

Meghan's fingers gripped the armrest of Alex's Ford pickup as he chased the setting sun down the West Texas farm road. Six hours ago, she'd hopped on a plane bound for the Lone Star state and the man she'd fallen in love with. Three months of daily Skype calls, emails and text messages had revealed she'd found a man who completely loved her as thoroughly as she loved him. And a man who made her feel worthy of being loved. But even that knowledge didn't change the fact that it had been a long time since she'd felt so…terrified.

He grabbed her hand and squeezed her fingers. "You're not regretting coming to meet my family, are you?"

She forced a smile. "Of course not."

Because she really wasn't. Not regretting coming to be with him, at least. It was just the idea of meeting Alex's three sisters, their spouses and children, along with his father—the patriarch of the family—that had her ready to hop back on a plane to Southern California.

"Then what is it? You've hardly said a word the past fifty miles."

She slipped off her sunglasses and set them on her head as the sun dropped toward the horizon, leaving behind a pinkish-orange glow. "I'm just a little nervous."

"You have nothing to worry about. I promise. They're going to love you."

"Just understand that family gatherings in my household—which were rare—usually meant a movie at the mall and Chinese takeout with my father. He only had one, unmarried sister, so I never had aunts and uncles and dozens of cousins, much less siblings of my own."

"You're going to be fine." He shot her a smile, then pulled off at the next exit and started following the dusty road north. "Trust me."

She shouldn't worry, and she knew it. If she could survive eight-plus months in the African bush stalking lions and being kidnapped by poachers and left for dead, surely she could handle meeting his family. But still…

"There is one other small thing." He glanced at her, still holding her hand. "I talked to my sister Julia while I waited for your plane to land."

Great. "Something else for me to worry about?"

"No, it's just that there are going to be a few more people at the house this weekend than I originally thought."

Which meant more names and faces to remember.

"Turns out my father's two sisters and their husbands arrive tomorrow, though they'll all be sleeping in town."

He'd told her earlier that the nearest town boasted a population of 576 people, a café with the best pecan pie in the county and two traffic lights. She'd be staying at the ranch, rooming with his sister Camy and his fifteen-year-old niece, Heather.

Meghan searched her memory for his aunts' names. "Barbara and…Gina?"

"Gail."

"Okay." She drew in a deep breath in an attempt to calm her nerves. What were two more couples?

"Barbara's married to Barry, who recently retired from the military. They spend most of the year traveling in their forty-foot motor home. Gail's married to Jim. They live in New York, but have been in Amarillo the past two weeks, staying with their daughter and son-in-law, who just had a baby."

She was never going to remember everyone's name. "You require name tags at family reunions, right?"

He laughed. "Far as I know, none of their children will be coming, so this will actually be a small event."

Small?

"At the last Markham family reunion," he said, "over a hundred and fifty showed up."

A hundred and fifty? She couldn't even imagine fifty. Butterflies stirred in her stomach. Maybe she'd spent too much time soaking up the quiet of the African bush. She stared out the window, hoping the endless miles of open land surrounding them, broken up only by occasional outcroppings of rocks and patches of brush, would help calm her nerves.

"It is beautiful out here."

"Remind you of the African bush?" Alex asked.

"In some ways, yes, except for the paved road with its perfectly painted yellow line down the middle."

He laughed. "That and the lack of a lion pride or any elephants lumbering across the horizon."

"Just mountain lions and those unpredictable wild boars?"

"Do you miss it?"

"Every day. I miss the quiet of sitting and waiting for Kibibi to appear, drinking tea while watching the sunset and the brilliance of the night stars. I miss Nathi, Kate and Samuel. What I don't miss, though, is running for my life from some international crime syndicate."

"Me, neither." He squeezed her hand. "But we don't need wild animals and poachers to keep things exciting here. I've got three meddling sisters and a passel of nieces and nephews that keep life interesting."

"Wait a minute. Five minutes ago, you were assuring me how wonderful your family is. Now it sounds as if you're trying to scare me off."

"Never." Alex laughed. "They might end up driving you crazy, and you'll eat more Tex-Mex and barbecue than you ever thought possible, but they're a family who will have your back every time." Nervous as she was, she had to admit that sounded wonderful.

Fifteen minutes later, Alex parked at the end of La Bella Raina's dusty driveway. There was just enough light left to wash the two-story ranch house in the hazy golds of the sunset. Meghan stepped out of the truck, breathed in a mixture of hay and the woodsy scent of a fireplace and felt her shoulders relax.

"Wow. This is stunning."

"And you haven't even seen the inside yet." He took her hand and headed for the house. "Come on in and meet everyone. I'll bring in your suitcase later."

Meghan walked beside him toward the house with its stone walls, huge picture windows and long veranda. Despite her fears of meeting his family, there was also a measure of peace in her about being here. They'd both taken time over the past few weeks to chase away the lingering shadows from their pasts.

She'd met her father in Cape Town and spent a week with him, facing long-buried issues from the past, learning to forgive and working on building a new relationship for their future. At the same time, Alex had visited his grandparents' homestead and his mother's grave, bring closure to a piece of his personal history he would always carry with him.

He turned to her on the veranda, pulled her into his arms and kissed her before they stepped into the house.

Her heart took a nosedive. "What was that for?"

"To make sure you know I love you and can't imagine bringing anyone else home to meet my family."

Meghan smiled as they walked through the front door, across the shiny wood floors, finally stopping in front of an extraordinary fireplace. They stood there for a moment, taking in the tangy smell of barbecue and noisy laughter from the back of the house.

"Anybody home?"

An older man using a carved wooden cane met them. Tall, broad shoulders, graying dark hair… She'd recognize Alex's father anywhere. "Mr. Markham."

"Please." The older man's smile widened. "*Mr. Markham* sounds way too formal. Call me Charles."

Alex placed a protective arm around her. "Dad, this is Meghan."

"So I finally get to meet the woman who captured my only son's heart."

Before Meghan could respond, the room was filled with the buzz of excited chatter.

"It's taken you long enough to get her here. I'm Camy, Alex's youngest older sister." She gathered Meghan into a big hug. "I can't tell you how excited I am to meet you."

"I'm glad to meet you, too—"

"Have you ever been horseback riding?"

"What about hunting? Uncle Alex, could we go hunting tomorrow?"

Meghan tried to field the questions from two boys with bright red hair and freckles sprinkled across their noses.

"Or swimming if it's not too cold. Do you like to swim?"

"Boys, where are your manners?" asked another woman who could only be Sara. "Introduce yourself before you swamp Meghan with all of your questions. There'll be time for all of that tomorrow, but for now, both your uncle and Meghan are tired."

Meghan couldn't help but smile. "You must be… Tyler and Cameron."

"He's Cameron and I'm Tyler. Uncle Alex's favorite nephew." Tyler shot his uncle a broad grin.

"You're not his favorite," Cameron countered as Alex drew them both into a bear hug.

"Boys!" Sara shook her head and apologized to Meghan. "They're excited."

"They have every right to be excited. It isn't every day that Alex brings home a girl."

"I heard that, Heather." Alex gave his niece a big hug.

"Personally, I'm glad to hear it isn't a common occurrence." Meghan took in all the energy and excitement around her. Nervous or not, this was what she'd always wanted. A big family with traditions, laughter and, yes, even the inevitable drama. Meghan laughed, then turned to the teenage girl. "I hear we're going to be roommates for the weekend."

"Yes, and Grandpa is giving us the master bedroom. It's huge with a Jacuzzi tub—you're going to love it!"

"Looks like someone is trying to impress our guest, Dad."

"And why not? It's about time you found someone to settle down with."

"I agree. I'm Julia, mother of three precocious little girls who are currently having a tea party upstairs, but will be tearing through here any moment." Julia linked her arm with Meghan's. "I'll be the first to admit that we're a bit overwhelming at first, but hopefully you'll come to love us."

Any fear Meghan had felt was quickly dissipating. "I know I will."

"Are you tired?" Camy asked.

"Not really. I dozed a bit on the flight."

"Good, hopefully you're hungry, because dinner is almost ready."

"Can I help?"

"You bet." The women started back toward the kitchen. "We can always use an extra hand, and maybe you can tell us firsthand some of your adventures in South Africa."

Alex grabbed her hand and smiled at her. "I told you they'd love you."

A moment later, Meghan stepped into a kitchen bigger than her entire chalet back in South Africa. She couldn't remember the last time she'd actually cooked something.

"Would you mind frying up the rest of the okra, Meghan?" Julia scooted past her with a bag of flour. "I need to get the gravy finished for the chicken-fried steak."

A buzzer went off over the stove.

"Sara, that's your pie," someone shouted.

"Got it."

Meghan turned to a pile of sliced green okra while the rest of the women fluttered around the kitchen like Martha Stewart. "Okra…"

Camy must have caught the look of panic in her

eyes, because she swooped in, arm around Meghan, and steered her toward the dining room.

"Heather, take over the okra, will you? I need Meghan's help to get the table set." Camy grabbed a basket of silverware on the way. "You don't mind, do you? It was getting too crowded in the kitchen."

"Actually, you just saved me." They stepped into the dining room with its high ceiling and rustic wood beams that held a table built to hold at least a dozen and a card table set up on the side, presumably for the kids. "Cooking isn't exactly my specialty."

"Mine, either." Camy handed her a stack of white dinner plates from a wooden hutch. "I've always pre-ferred the outdoors to a stuffy kitchen."

Fifteen minutes later, she'd met the brothers-in-law and Julia's three girls, and was sitting in front of a spread the size of Texas—barbecued ribs, chicken-fried steak, corn on the cob, beans, fried okra and a sideboard of desserts.

As soon as the amens had been said, the questions started again. Where had she grown up? What was her favorite animal on safari? When would they be able to watch her documentary on the internet? Was she going to make another documentary? Had she ever had a pet monkey or lion or giraffe? Meghan fielded the ques-tions while filling her plate.

"What I want to know about is how you managed to survive being kidnapped by some international crime syndicate," Camy said.

"It was scary, but thankfully, there was this Texas Ranger who saved my life." Meghan squeezed Alex's hand under the table. Meeting his family was turning out to be tame compared to what she'd gone through those last few days.

Cameron jumped up from the kids' table to grab a roll from their bread basket. "Mama says you're getting married, Uncle Alex. Is that true?"

The table went silent. Meghan looked to Alex.

"Cameron, I—" Alex pushed a piece of fried okra across his plate.

"Cameron, that isn't the kind of question you ask a couple in public," Sara said.

"Especially before the man has proposed," Alex added.

Cameron frowned. "I would have asked in private, but there are too many people here."

Someone snickered. Meghan shifted in her chair.

"Sorry. I was just curious." Cameron started back to his table.

Alex cleared his throat, then tapped a knife against one of the glasses to get everyone's attention. The room fell completely silent as a dozen pairs of eyes stared at them.

"Meghan, Cameron might have spoken out of turn, but he was right that I have a question to ask you."

Meghan gulped in a breath of air. Surely he wasn't proposing now? She looked down the row of faces she'd all just met. Sisters, brothers-in-law, nieces and nephews... This wasn't exactly how she'd imagined him proposing. She'd daydreamed about a quiet table for two while the African sun splashed its golds and oranges across the horizon, or even here at the family ranch sprawled out on a blanket beneath a tree with a picnic basket and nothing but the West Texas sky for miles and miles.

Certainly not in front of his entire family.

"Maybe this isn't the perfect moment I'd planned," he continued, "but I've been thinking about this for a long time. About you and me and our future."

Meghan dropped her fork onto her plate and scooted her chair back as Alex knelt down beside her. His hands shook as he grasped them. He really was going to propose.

Someone let out a whoop from the end of the table. Meghan felt her cheeks heat up.

"I had something prepared for you—something I'd planned to share with you in private." Alex shot a glance at Cameron. "But I'm not sure I can wait until we have a moment alone. Or for that matter, if we'll ever have a moment alone. So I hope you'll forgive me, because I'm not exactly one for making speeches."

"Just tell her how you feel," someone called out.

Someone else giggled in the background, but Meghan barely heard it. All she could see was Alex, on his knees, getting ready to ask her to marry him.

"When I decided to take the assignment in Africa," he said, "I went to find that hole my mother left when she died. To heal and to find a way to escape my own burnout. Instead, I found what I was really looking for all along. You."

Meghan felt her heart tremble. Everyone around them melted away. All she could see was the man she'd fallen in love with, looking up at her with those gorgeous eyes of his that made her heart flutter like a teenager's again. The man who had filled the missing pieces inside her own heart.

Tears welled in her eyes as he continued.

"The time I spent visiting my mother's home after I left you confirmed all the things I felt while we were together. And those feelings deepened during these weeks we've been apart, making me realize just how much I love you. You were the one who made me laugh again. Showed me how to find peace again. Showed me that I didn't need more religion, but instead more love for my Savior and those around me. Showed me that pursing justice is still worth fighting for. So I spoke to your father last night and asked his permission to marry you."

"Uh-oh," someone called out.

"He gave me his permission, Camy," Alex said with a mock glare at his sister.

Meghan tried not to cry as he pulled out a small black velvety box from his pocket.

"Like the ranch that belongs to our family, this was my mother's ring and my grandmother's before that."

He opened the box and pulled out the simple, beautiful solitary-diamond ring.

"Meghan Alyssa Jordan, will you marry me?"

Her heart pounded as he slipped the ring onto her finger. "Yes."

"Kiss her…kiss her…" someone started chanting in the background.

Alex laughed as he pulled her into his arms. She lost herself in his kiss. She was no longer the little girl searching for love and family, because for the first time in as long as she could remember, she'd finally come home.

* * * * *

Dear Reader,

I had so much fun writing this story because it brought together many of the things I've loved about living in Africa over the past ten years, from the people to the animals to the scenic beauty. This continent has captured a piece of my heart, and I'm thrilled for the opportunity to give you a glimpse of this beautiful place. One of my favorite things to do is go on safari. My family and I have been able to see so many amazing things, and for me, each animal, each sunset and the vast night sky really do "declare the glory of God." The other thing that has impacted my life is the people I've been able to meet. They've taught me how to laugh, love, dream and how to truly give from the heart.

Be blessed,
Lisa Harris

Questions for Discussion

1. We've all had people in our lives who have let us down and hurt us, but forgiveness doesn't always come easy. What have you learned in life on how to forgive and let go?

2. Is there a specific person in your own life you still need to forgive? If so, what is a tangible way you can move forward in letting go of this hurt?

3. Kate tells Meghan that she had to continually remind herself that her identity isn't "determined by who I'm with, but by the One who created me." What do you think about that statement?

4. When Kate asks Meghan what makes her push Alex away, Meghan admits he makes her feel vulnerable. Have you missed out on things because you felt vulnerable?

5. What measuring tool should you use to measure your self-worth? What people say about you, or what God says about you?

6. I'd love the chance to do a wildlife documentary and spend a few weeks filming in the bush. What is a dream that you have that you've yet to realize?

7. Alex realizes that many people believe that the end justifies the means. He also sees that money can turn someone away from the truth and break their

integrity. What do you think about that statement, and how can we avoid falling into that trap?

8. James says in the Bible that pure religion is to look after the orphans and widows and keep ourselves from being polluted from the earth. How do you think this verse should apply to our own lives?

9. What do you think about this statement: "It doesn't matter what is true. What matters is what is believed."

10. Do you come from a big family or a small family? How did that influence your growing up?

11. If you were able to go on a safari, what animals would you like to see?

12. Meghan loves to travel in this story. If you could travel anywhere in the world, where would you go?

REQUEST YOUR FREE BOOKS!
2 FREE RIVETING INSPIRATIONAL NOVELS
PLUS 2 FREE MYSTERY GIFTS

Love Inspired ®
SUSPENSE

YES! Please send me 2 FREE Love Inspired® Suspense novels and my 2 FREE mystery gifts (gifts are worth about $10). After receiving them, if I don't wish to receive any more books, I can return the shipping statement marked "cancel." If I don't cancel, I will receive 4 brand-new novels every month and be billed just $4.74 per book in the U.S. or $5.24 per book in Canada. That's a savings of at least 21% off the cover price. It's quite a bargain! Shipping and handling is just 50¢ per book in the U.S. and 75¢ per book in Canada.* I understand that accepting the 2 free books and gifts places me under no obligation to buy anything. I can always return a shipment and cancel at any time. Even if I never buy another book, the two free books and gifts are mine to keep forever.

123/323 IDN F5AC

Name	(PLEASE PRINT)	
Address		Apt. #
City	State/Prov.	Zip/Postal Code

Signature (if under 18, a parent or guardian must sign)

Mail to the **Harlequin® Reader Service:**
IN U.S.A.: P.O. Box 1867, Buffalo, NY 14240-1867
IN CANADA: P.O. Box 609, Fort Erie, Ontario L2A 5X3

**Are you a current subscriber to Love Inspired Suspense books
and want to receive the larger-print edition?
Call 1-800-873-8635 or visit www.ReaderService.com.**

* Terms and prices subject to change without notice. Prices do not include applicable taxes. Sales tax applicable in N.Y. Canadian residents will be charged applicable taxes. Offer not valid in Quebec. This offer is limited to one order per household. Not valid for current subscribers to Love Inspired Suspense books. All orders subject to credit approval. Credit or debit balances in a customer's account(s) may be offset by any other outstanding balance owed by or to the customer. Please allow 4 to 6 weeks for delivery. Offer available while quantities last.

Your Privacy—The Harlequin® Reader Service is committed to protecting your privacy. Our Privacy Policy is available online at www.ReaderService.com or upon request from the Harlequin Reader Service.
We make a portion of our mailing list available to reputable third parties that offer products we believe may interest you. If you prefer that we not exchange your name with third parties, or if you wish to clarify or modify your communication preferences, please visit us at www.ReaderService.com/consumerchoice or write to us at Harlequin Reader Service Preference Service, P.O. Box 9062, Buffalo, NY 14269. Include your complete name and address.

LIS13R

SPECIAL EXCERPT FROM

Love Inspired
SUSPENSE

Morgan Smith is hiding in the Witness Protection Program. Has her past come back to haunt her?

Read on for a preview of
TOP SECRET IDENTITY by Sharon Dunn,
the next exciting book in the
WITNESS PROTECTION series
from Love Inspired Suspense. Available April 2014.

A wave of terror washed over Morgan Smith when she heard the tapping at her window. Someone was outside the caretaker's cottage. Had the man who'd tried to kill her in Mexico found her in Iowa?

Though she'd been in witness protection for two months, her fear of being killed had never subsided. She'd left Des Moines for the countryside and a job at a stable because she had felt exposed in the city, vulnerable. She'd grown up on a ranch in Wyoming, and when she'd worked as an American missionary in Mexico, she'd always chosen to be in rural areas. Wide-open spaces seemed safer to her.

With her heart pounding, she rose to her feet and walked the short distance to the window, half expecting to see a face contorted with rage, or clawlike hands reaching for her neck. The memory of nearly being strangled made her shudder. She stepped closer to the window, seeing only blackness. Yet the sound of the tapping had been too distinct to dismiss as the wind rattling the glass.

A chill snaked down her spine.

Someone was outside.

If the man from Mexico had come to kill her, it seemed odd that he would give her a warning by tapping on the window.

She thought to call her new boss, who was in the guesthouse less than a hundred yards away. Alex Reardon seemed like a nice man. She'd hated being evasive when he'd asked her where she had gotten her knowledge of horses. She'd been blessed to get the job without references. Her references, everything and everyone she knew, all of that had been stripped from her, even her name. She was no longer Magdalena Chavez. Her new name was Morgan Smith.

The knob on the locked door turned and rattled.

She'd been a fool to think the U.S. Marshals could keep her safe.

Pick up TOP SECRET IDENTITY wherever
Love Inspired® Suspense books and ebooks are sold.

Carl King scraped most of the mud off his boots and walked up to the front door of his boss's home. Joe Shetler had gone to purchase straw from a neighbor, but he would be back soon. After an exhausting morning spent struggling to pen and doctor one ornery and stubborn ewe, Carl had rounded up half the remaining sheep and moved them closer to the barns with the help of his dog, Duncan.

He opened the front door and stopped dead in his tracks. An Amish woman stood at the kitchen sink. She had her back to him as she rummaged for something. She hadn't heard him come in.

He resisted the intense impulse to rush back outside. He didn't like being shut inside with anyone. He fought his growing discomfort. This was Joe's home. This woman didn't belong here.

"What are you doing?" he demanded.

She shrieked and whirled around to face him. "You scared the life out of me."

He clenched his fists and stared at his feet. "I didn't mean to frighten you. Who are you and what are you doing here?"

"Who are you? You're not Joseph Shetler. I was told this was Joseph's house."

She was a slender little thing. The top of her head wouldn't reach his chin unless she stood on tiptoe. She was dressed Plain in a drab faded green calf-length dress with a matching cape and apron. Her hair, on the other hand, was anything but drab. It was ginger-red, and wisps of it curled near her temples. The rest was hidden beneath the black *kapp* she wore.

He didn't recognize her, but she could be a local. He made a point of avoiding people, so it wasn't surprising that he didn't know her.

"I'm sorry. My name is Elizabeth Barkman. People call me Lizzie. I'm Joe's granddaughter from Indiana."

As far as Carl knew, Joe didn't have any family. "Joe doesn't have a granddaughter, and he doesn't like people in his house."

"Actually, he has four granddaughters. I can see why he doesn't like to have people in. This place is a mess. He certainly could use a housekeeper. I know an excellent one who is looking for a position."

Pick up THE SHEPHERD'S BRIDE
wherever Love Inspired® books and ebooks are sold.